the QUEEN OF ESCAPES

AIRSHIP 27 PRODUCTIONS

The Queen of Escapes
© 2013 Curtis Fernlund

Published by Airship 27 Productions
www.airship27.com
www.airship27hangar.com

Interior illustrations © 2013 James Lyle
Cover illustration © 2013 Andy Fish

Editor: Ron Fortier
Associate Editor: Charles Saunders
Production and design by Rob Davis
Promotions and marketing by Michael Vance

ISBN-13: 978-0615903866
ISBN-10: 061590386X

Printed in the United States of America

10 9 8 7 6 5 4 3 2 1

CURTIS FERNLUND

This book is dedicated to Jane.

Episode One:
Queen of Escapes!

Brazil
1935

*G*loria Swann ran for all she was worth…

Her breath was coming out in ragged gasps as her legs churned furiously, driving her forward through the dense green foliage of the jungle. Her feet hurt, as her boots seemed too tight, the lacings biting into her ankles, and the trail through the jungle was barely a rock strewn path not fit for a goat let alone a person. Every step was agony. The sun was beating down, even though it was low in the sky, almost touching the horizon and mostly hidden through the thick verdant tapestry of the surrounding trees. Every breath was strained in the hot humid air that was thick with mosquitoes and other vile insect swarms that bit and stung and made her day to day existence miserable. Gloria Swann hated the jungle in particular and South America in general. Brazil most specifically. She wanted to go home.

She burst from the dense rain forest at last in a shower of leaves, the trail arching off and away across a small clearing. Not far off towards her left she could see the river that she had been pacing, barely a dozen yards away. She could hear the roar of the water, her eyes searching ahead to where the land seemed to drop away over the edge of a cliff and the falls cascading beyond, her destination at long last.

The heat seemed to double as she staggered into the clearing; the setting sun blazing down on her now and searing her sweat-sheened skin, the meager protection of the jungle left behind. Gloria felt the perspiration rolling down her body, making her shirt cling to her and stinging at her eyes, matting her hair to her dirty cheeks and neck. The open air was just as thick with insects as the forest had been, and a huge bird soared far overhead watching her race, laughing at her with its raucous call. Another time and she might stop and marvel at the creature, as even at a glance it seemed magnificent and beautiful as it drifted lazily in the heated air held aloft by huge, wide wings. But not now… not today. She had no time to waste, dreaming and sight seeing. Gloria had to reach the cliff.

To make matters worse, as though the trials of the damnable jungle were not enough, her hands were bound uncomfortably behind her back, tied loosely with a coarse, woven rope. The binding held her arms back at an awkward angle, and made running all the harder because of it. The ropes did not hurt really, not too much anyway, but they were an inconvenience. She could not even wipe the perspiration from her brow.

Suddenly she heard the screams and shouts of her pursuers and Gloria's heart leapt into her throat. She dared not glance back to see just how far behind her they were, lest she stumble on the uneven rocky trail, but she felt sure that they were almost upon her, dogging her heels. They sounded an angry mob, and she knew that they were all far younger than she was, and in much better shape, and would catch her in no time if she did not reach the cliff's edge. Gloria had no doubts that she was out of shape, if not just a tad over weight. And much as she was loathe to admit it, at just over forty, she knew that she was no longer a spring chicken. The race had taken a Herculean effort on her part, and she was ready to collapse.

She stumbled along, tears streaming down her face now as she pushed herself even harder. The path wound towards the water, as the cliff drew closer with every stride. An arrow plunged into the path ahead of her, but far closer than she would have liked. She let out a shrill little gasp of surprise, lifting her legs higher as the shouts grew behind her.

Gloria slowed her pace, almost sliding in the gravel and loose dirt at the edge of the cliff as she came to a halt. She peered over the precipice, watching as hundreds and thousands of gallons of water rushed over the falls, now just a few feet away, plunging fast and furious over fifty feet to the raging pool below. The noise was deafening as she inched forward, staring out at the river that continued its course vanishing finally as the jungle canopy closed over it in the distance. She felt a twinge of vertigo, swaying slightly as she watched the thundering cascade rush and roar on and on. She swallowed, jumping in surprise as another arrow dug into the dirt near her feet, just a few inches away. Too damn close!

"And…Cut! That's a print! Stand in! You're up! Get ready!"

Gloria Swann spun about at the director's shouts and glared at the eight women that were jogging casually to a stop some dozen yards back up the path. She hated them! They were all almost half her age and gorgeous, with long muscular legs and taut tanned bodies. Their hair was all long and thick and full, framing their oval and perfectly handsome faces. Their costumes, little more than rags and animal skins, only made them look all the more exotic and enticing. They were barely sweating, but their perspiration glistened, enhancing their beauty for God's sake!

"Who fired that last arrow?" Gloria snapped, her skin flushing with the heat and burning with fury as she rotated her arms and wrists, twisting her hands free of the loosely tied cords that bound them. She eyed the beauties as they all dumbly looked from one to the other, but none spoke up and confessed. "C'mon! Who was it?"

Gloria stormed forward, her eyes crackling, angling towards three that held the small wooden props that were little more than toy bows. The other women that were holding longer sticks done up to look like spears and blow guns all eased back to give the movie star room. They knew better than to get in the way when Gloria Swann, Queen of Escapes, was on the warpath.

Gloria stared at the three, ignoring the fright that her hair must be and the sweat dripping down her face and back. She was still breathing hard, but she used her will to control it as she tossed the now useless rope aside. She would be damned if she would let this trio of...of *extras* get the better of her. For their part, the three young actresses, dressed sparingly in animal skins that barely covered their more private parts and held their ample bosoms in check, all blushed and looked away, suddenly more interested in the dirt at their feet than in anything that Gloria Swann had to say.

"All right!" Gloria almost shrieked. "Which of you three fired that last arrow? Was it you?" Gloria jabbed a finger at a statuesque blonde, her long hair pulled back into a ponytail. The blonde woman turned a deeper shade of red, but shook her head, mumbling that she was innocent. Gloria scowled and glared at the other two. They could not meet her gaze. That was good. Gloria's scowl quickly turned into a conceited sneer.

"Fine!" she snapped, crossing her arms over her own adequate, if sagging only a bit, bosom. "None of you wants to confess, then you're *all* fired! I'll tell Jonathan now, and you'll all be let go! I'll teach you all to fire arrows too close to me, and the rest of you better learn!" The trio of beauties all stared at the movie star with open-mouthed shock, gasping and moaning in dismay. The other women had moved out of the line of fire, but not so far so they could not hear, and they all mumbled under their breath when Gloria turned on them. "I'm the star of this film! Not any of you! And none of you better forget it!"

Gloria raised her chin defiantly and stormed away, actually shouldering through the trio of women too dumbstruck to move. She spied the film's director, Jonathan Harkins sitting in his high canvas-backed chair going over the script, and veered towards him, lifting her tight, khaki skirt to better watch the rocky path before her. She would burn in hell before she put up with any of this stupidity any longer. A few inches to the left and that last arrow might have hit her. She might have been hurt, or worse! Despite her age, Gloria Swann was still a big star in Hollywood, and a big draw at the box office. She would have her way, and those bims would all be sacked. And anyone else that got in her way!

Gloria looked up making sure that Harkins was still in place, and gasped. Again, as she had so many times before, she stared in amazement at the young woman walking casually towards her. Angela Morgan, Gloria's stand in was almost fifteen years younger than the aging star, but she was the spitting image of what Gloria had once been years ago. They were dressed the same, in a khaki canvas knee length skirt and thick blouse with high brown leather boots that laced up to the knee. Their hair was styled and cut all but identical, a dirty brown, though Gloria's was streaked with sweat and plastered to her head while Angela's was colored slightly to hide a white streak that touched her crown. But even their faces were remarkably alike, with the same full lips and dark green eyes, the same oval shape with high cheekbones and a small, pert nose. For Gloria, it was like looking into a magic mirror to see herself, as she had been a decade before; young and beautiful. She could only imagine what the Morgan girl saw and thought in return, looking at her.

They passed on the trail, the younger woman smiling and nodding as Gloria raised her chin a bit higher and stared down her nose at her stand in. Angela had been hired to do those things deemed too dangerous for Gloria, or too strenuous, or simply too mundane and not worthy of the star's greater talents. Angela Morgan was likable enough, Gloria supposed, and she did her job well, but she had airs like the rest of the rabble. Gloria felt it was her duty to keep the little people in their collective places, and she did so with a relish.

"Make sure you show off my good side this time, dear." Gloria smirked, strutting towards the director's chair, hearing her stunt double sigh.

"That would be your big, fat butt, right?" Angela mumbled, watching the wicked witch of East Hollywood stalk off to make some other poor soul's life miserable, glad that it was not her that had attracted the movie star's ire this time.

Angela wondered what had happened in her life that had made the woman such an arrogant snob. Fifteen years ago Angela Morgan had idolized the great Gloria Swann. She had loved going to the Saturday matinee, seeing a Buster Keaton or Charlie Chaplin comedy, or a Gloria Swann adventure serial. She would become immersed in the action, staring wide-eyed as Gloria would outwit the Kaiser's bumbling soldiers, or some native tribe in Africa, or even a gang of mobsters or boot-leggers in America. Angela had known even back then, living in New York's Hell's Kitchen that was what she wanted to be when she grew up; a movie star!

It was a quirk of fate, however, that had determined that Angela looked almost identical to her Silver Screen heroine when she had finally grown old enough to try her own hand at acting. She had taken a bus across country, to a bustling, growing Hollywood filled with aspiring young actors and actresses like herself, only to find out that even though she was an adequate talent, she bore too close a resemblance to the then leading star. Time and again she was turned away with the sometimes not so polite refusal, that she would never get more than a bit part, at least as long as Gloria Swann was still on top of the Hollywood heap.

Finally, at the suggestion of her acting coach, she had applied to be Gloria's understudy at the film production company where Gloria was contracted. It seemed her only choice, to follow her dream at least in some respect, and not have to return home in defeat and disgrace. Oddly however, she found that she enjoyed working as Gloria's stand in, and she was hired immediately, making more money than she would have ever dreamed possible. Not only was she almost the spitting younger image of her favorite movie star, but as Angela was honing her acting skills, so too was she learning the arts of female escapology. Growing up and marveling at the escapades of Harry Houdini she had spent hours bound and gagged by her very own brother and some of her closer friends; struggling with the knots and cords binding her, learning all the tricks to free herself again from every possible situation that she could imagine. She had been hog-tied and bound to poles and pillars. She had been tied and locked away in basements and closets. She had been hung by her arms until they were aching so badly that she would cry, but she always managed to escape. In many ways, she knew more than Gloria herself. And Gloria's claim to fame was that she was the Queen of Escapes.

So, for almost five years Angela had done the dangerous and daring work that was deemed too much and too dangerous for the aging movie star. Angela was the one who was bound and gagged and thrown into perilous situations with Gloria mugging for the close-ups and doing the more tame and intimate scenes. Gloria got to kiss the hero, and receive the adulation of the crowd while Angela did all the real work. And for the most part, Angela loved it. While other women might resent always living in the shadow of another, Angela relished it. She was doing what she had wanted to do for so long, getting paid and living better than anyone of her family or friends ever had. And she was having fun.

Angela Morgan twisted her wrists, checking the special rope bonds that held her hands and arms behind her back for at least the twentieth time as she walked towards the cliff and her mark. Like Gloria, she had been loosely bound, but her own ropes were actually tied into knots and not just looped about her wrists and held in place. The cords were different though; a special line that had been cut and hollowed out a bit, just an inch or so, at the severed ends, with the hollowed parts then filled with a short, thin stick of wood that would hold the two halves together until Angela applied enough strength to separate them. Angela had heard that the great Harry Houdini used something similar in his act, and she had gotten Karl the Prop Manager and Stunt Coordinator to create something like that for her. Simply by pulling her arms, the rope would separate and she would be free enough to undo the loops of the cord and escape. It was so simple, it was positively brilliant.

Angela stepped right up to the cliff's edge and peered over the lip of the precipice. She watched as the great plume of never-ending water from the river streamed over the edge, plunging almost fifty feet into the large deep pool below. It was not such a long drop. She had leapt from higher, but it was not the fall that was the stunt in this instance. Some thirty feet below where she stood, Angela spied the rope that was strung across the gorge, camouflaged with moss and leaves, disguised as a passable vine.

Her job would be to leap from the cliff to escape her Amazonian pursuers, or rather, Gloria's pursuers, escape from the ropes binding her wrists as she fell, grab the 'vine' and then swing out to safety far down the river. Not an impossible task, but one that left little margin for error. Still, as her gaze followed the disguised rope arching out over the water and disappearing into the thick branches of a large tree that loomed over the pool below, she was confident that she was safe. She trusted Karl Braun, the prop manager and stunt coordinator, as she preferred to call him, and knew that the rope would be securely tied to the tree and that it had been measured to the inch to set her safely on the river bank far below after the arch of her swing. Karl had been the one to bind her, in fact, and he made doubly certain that her trick rope was in perfect working order. She would simply have to tug on her bonds and then swing the trailing rope under her legs to get her hands back in front of her. Then she must grab the rope and it would swing her to safety. The only real hazard of the stunt was getting her hands in front of her quickly enough, and leaping out far enough to grab at the rope in time. Angela would be jumping without the benefit of much of a running start, thanks mainly to Gloria's fear of heights. The actress insisted that she stop well away from the edge of the cliff to ensure her own safety, and Angela would have to leap from where she stopped. It was a twenty-foot arching jump, and Angela was just a little worried that she might not make it.

Angela looked at the ground, inspecting the area around the edge of the cliff, kicking away a few of the larger pieces of rock littering the ground at her feet. She frowned to see Gloria's foot prints over ten feet away from where she was standing. Gloria had missed her mark, and as Angela walked to where the star had stood, she could see that the extra distance placed the leap to the rope well outside the limits of safety. Even if she got her hands free, she would never make that extra distance in her leap and grab the vine.

Angela sighed, hoping that the cameras would not show the difference after editing. She had to leap from her mark, or the stunt would be ruined. She would miss the vine, or land in the wrong spot, or worse. She hated that it would not be perfect, but there was no way that she might do the stunt from where Gloria had stopped. She hoped that Jonathan, the director would not notice, or at least would understand.

Peering over the edge of the cliff again, Angela could just make out the silhouette of the safety boat hidden in the shadows of the thick foliage at the river's bank and the roiling mists created by the waterfall. She knew that Karl was in the boat, waiting to drag her from the water should anything go wrong with the stunt, or if she should get injured somehow. She could also see one of the three cameras that would be trained on her for the fall. Three cameras were almost unheard of in an on site adventure serial, but Gloria herself had backed this venture, along with several producers, and the budget apparently allowed for the extra expense of getting all the stunts from as many angles as possible. Along with the camera situated down on the river bank below, there was also one set on a platform amongst the trees further down river and the third would be trained on her from behind to get the image of her leap over the precipice. There were too many people involved with just this shot for Angela to get it wrong, and she had to admit that she was becoming a little anxious for it all to be over.

Angela turned at the shrill screech of Gloria Swann's voice as it cut across the set. She saw the actress in the midst of the production crew surrounding Jonathan Harkins as he sat in his high wooden director's chair. Gloria seemed to be fuming, shaking her finger almost in Harkin's face and gesturing wildly at the extras that were milling about at their marks a few yards away. All around the director, his staff busily tried to do their respective jobs; the script girl thumbed through her copy of the day's scenes, the head camera coordinator peered through a small view finder, trying to measure the remaining light for the final shot of the day, the make-up girl tried to swab the sweat away from Gloria's brow, only to be swatted away. For his part, Harkins stared at Gloria, apparently listening intently through her tirade though Angela knew differently. The Assistant Director, John Thomas, was leaning in closely behind Harkins, his lips moving, and Angela knew that whatever he was saying was far more important than anything that the arrogant star had to dispute. Angela had to smile.

Angela glanced over at the eight women who made up the pack of Gloria's pursuers. They were all drop-dead gorgeous, done up to look like Amazonian warriors from legend to fit in with the theme of the movie being shot. The gist of the story was that Gloria was an archeological explorer, riding the crest of popularity rising from the discoveries of ancient tombs found in Egypt over the past few years. Her character would discover a hidden, forgotten city deep in the dense jungles of South America, rich with gold and jewels and populated by fierce female warriors; the Amazons. The film would then focus on Gloria's trials and tribulations as she tried to escape from the city and get back to civilization with some proof of her discoveries. As an adventure serial, it was a good plot with plenty of action written into the script. Gloria's own money and power made sure that she would come out on top, surrounded by exotic locations and the best direction and production that her wealth could buy. Finally, there would be dozens of beautiful and scantily clad women prancing about for the young men in the audience to ogle from week to week. Every episode would be tailor made to keep the crowds packing into the theatres and spending their hard-earned nickels and dimes.

The 'Amazons' looked bored and just a little abashed as they tried not to seem too interested at what Gloria Swann was saying. From what Angela could hear, Gloria seemed to be berating the extras, most specifically the trio that held the prop bows. One had fired an arrow a bit too close to Gloria it seemed, and she was furious. Angela giggled. The look on

Jonathan's face was priceless.

Angela could see the some of the extras smirking as well, though they were more able to hide their reactions than she was with her arms bound behind her back. She saw her friend, Jennifer Higgins, designated Third Amazon, trying desperately to stifle her own fit of giggles. The two friends locked eyes for a split second and both broke down in laughter. Jennifer covered her mouth and turned away, but all that Angela could do with her hands trapped behind her back was bite the inside of her cheek and hope that no one else took notice of her most unprofessional behavior. She took a step back, turning to face the falls again.

Something thumped into the dirt between her feet, startling her and she staggered. Glancing down Angela saw an arrow vibrating in the earth, and even as she gasped another struck, slicing through the thin leather of her boot and jutting from the dirt suddenly behind her ankle. She yelped in surprise and jumped back, the long wooden shaft snagging her boot and sending her off balance. Angela felt the ledge beneath her start to crumble under her sudden weight and give way.

Angela screamed!

Jonathan Harkins sighed trying his best to ignore the shrill ranting voice that was nagging at his ear like all the bugs in the jungle seemed to do. It seemed to be becoming almost a daily occurrence with the spoiled star. Gloria Swann had some new complaint every morning, and some suggestion or problem on almost every shot. Harkins swore that this would be the last film that he ever shared credit with the woman, and if not for the money she had promised the studio, he would not even be here in the steaming hell that was Brazil. It was not worth it…almost.

He looked up from his copy of the script that Shirley was holding for his perusal, pretending that he cared what Gloria Swann had to say. The sudden panicked cry had drawn his attention, and he glanced about quickly, hoping for anything that might distract Gloria from her latest tirade. His eyes went wide as they focused on the Morgan girl, Gloria's stand in, stumbling backwards towards the cliff's edge. His first thought was that she was in danger, that she needed help! But then he saw the waning light, and the possibility that the stunt would be ruined, and a day's shooting would be lost. More if the double was hurt, or killed of course.

Jonathan Harkins' mind raced in the space of a heartbeat. Even before the girl's scream began to fade and others about the set started to look up at the sudden commotion he was up and out of his chair. He shoved Gloria Swann out of his way, not even weighing the consequences of that abrupt action or the endless tirade of speeches he would have to endure later. He grabbed at his megaphone, shouting at Thomas his assistant as he ran forward.

"Action! Roll film! Roll film!!"

Everything seemed a blur as Angela fell backwards, but oddly, time seemed to slow as well, giving her a long hard look at what was happening. She saw the sudden stricken look of panic on Jennifer's face, her mouth opening wide, her breasts starting to strain at the skimpy strip of fur cloth that barely held them in place as she drew in breath to scream. She saw Harkins running forward, though not actually towards her. His megaphone slowly rose to his lips, the wide-mouthed cone hiding the look of startled determination on his face. She heard his booming voice barely over the roar of the cascading waterfalls calling for action. She saw Gloria Swann stumbling across the set, her footing lost and landing in a heap on the dirty trail.

Time caught up to itself as her heart slammed into her chest another beat. Angela's scream choked in her throat as she lost her view of the set, the edge of the precipice crumbling and falling away beneath her feet. Her stomach lurched at the sudden sensation that there was nothing under her anymore. Nothing to support her as gravity locked her in a vice-like grip and started to drag her down.

Down…

Angela screamed again!

EPISODE TWO:
THE FALLS OF DEATH!

*A*ngela Morgan's scream echoed about the gorge, piercing high and shrill above the roar of plummeting water. A horrible feeling of anxiety and panic gripped her body at the sudden sensation of weightlessness as the air seemed to open up around her. Her eyes grew wide as she realized that she was falling, possibly to her death.

She could hear the panicked shouts still coming from above. Her director, Jonathan Harkins voice loudest of all as he spurred the movie crew to life. A flitting thought, as Angela wondered why he was not screaming for someone to help her, rather than capture what might be her final plunge on film. More, she could hear the roar of the falls, thousands of gallons of water cascading over the edge of the precipice just as she was, just a few yards away, dropping almost fifty feet into the rocky churning pool below, quickly drowning out everything else.

As Angela's scream died in her throat, one anxiety was quickly replaced by another. Terror was pushed aside, and the will to live took over her body churning on adrenaline. She felt the cool spray of the waterfall washing over her even as grim determination washed over her face and set her brow. She kicked out as the face of the cliff rushed past, her feet ramming into the hard packed stone and dirt, her strong leg muscles pushing her falling body out and away farther over the seeming abyss.

Angela Morgan squirmed as her body arched out and down, tumbling and picking up speed in her ill-fated plunge. As a movie stunt woman she had been in falls before, but each had been different than the last. Every new fall seemed more and more dangerous; a little bit higher, a longer leap, or additional trappings added to complicate the stunt. Her fall today had been an almost standing jump out and away from the cliff's edge to grab at a concealed rope hanging far below and then to swing away to safety. All of that had gone out the window however after the pair of arrows had thudded into the ground at her feet, startling her over the edge, and now she struggled to survive, and if the shot worked, all the better.

Thus she found herself falling; her hands bound behind her back as the rocky, churning pool raced towards her, ever closer. Angela twisted her body, struggling to right herself even as she braced her body for impact just in case she could not get free. She struggled at the bonds as she squirmed, jerking and pulling at the special ropes that the stunt coordinator had earlier wrapped about her wrists and knotted off just so, giving the eye of the camera the effect that the pseudo Gloria Swann was seemingly helpless and doomed as she fell over the edge of the cliff. It was all staged for the camera, and seemingly safe for the stunt woman.

Someone had tried to kill her though, she was sure, and was doing a hell of a job. Angela kicked in the empty air as she fell, finally twisting her body into the proper position as she struggled at the bonds that held her wrists. She tugged at her bonds, the skin at her wrists pinching as the cord drew tight, the loosely tied loops closing. Her fingers danced over the cords, probing for the disguised break in the rope as the pool rose to greet her, expanding in her line of sight. She mumbled to herself, cursing under her breath as she fell, watching the rope disguised as a vine slowly looming ever closer below her, inch by inch. She needed her hands free and in front of her in order to save herself by grabbing that rope and swinging to safety before she hit the water and sank like a stone. Growing up in Hell's Kitchen, swimming had never been one of her strong points.

With a snarl and a straining of her muscles, Angela suddenly felt the rope binding her wrists loosen, the loops pulling apart and expanding. Quickly she brought her legs in with her knees up to her chin, curling her body into a tightly packed ball and stretching her arms to their limits. She screamed, hoping that she had enough slack in the rope to pass the cords beneath her derriere and heels. With her thighs pressing into her bosom and her arms straining, still she felt the rope graze her bottom as she forced her hands in front of her. Her body tumbled as the rope snagged on her heels, another second gone, another heartbeat closer to death.

And suddenly her hands were before her. Angela's wrists were still bound but there was almost a foot of cord between them now. She knew that the cameras would show that she was still securely bound as long as she kept her wrists together, and it would have looked that she had dramatically forced her arms before her to save herself. Only a few of Gloria's most ardent fans would notice the sudden additional length to the bonds, but even they would be happy if Angela made the stunt as dramatic as she possibly could.

Angela gasped as the rope that she was to grab finally came upon her. In the few seconds that had passed she had fallen almost two dozen feet, and her attention had been elsewhere. Angela stretched, thrusting her arms forward as she spread her body out as widely as it would go, hoping to slow her descent as much as she could in the remaining few seconds that she had. Groping, she reached out, the air whipping past her, the roar of the falls drowning out all but her own heartbeat thumping loudly in her ears. Her fingers clawed empty air for a second.

Two…

Angela closed her hands about the rope, her fists ripping off the leaves and moss that had been laced into the coarse weave as she slid trying to gain a grip. Friction burned and she felt her skin ripping away as her hands gained purchase. Her free fall abruptly halted as she changed direction and her body swung out and away towards the safety of the riverbank below.

Angela gritted her teeth against the sudden burning pain in her hands and shoulders, but still allowed a whimper to escape as her arms suddenly bore the weight of her body and the fall combined. She swung, an arch that jerked only a little as her fall had been altered from the initial jump. Karl Braun had set up the rope exactly, but her premature fall, despite her effort to push off of the cliff face had left her short. Her shoulders screamed in agony as her weight and speed of descent all forced down on her at once. She swung low, her toes actually trailing through the water of the churning pool before the rope drew up short and she was soaring up through the air again.

She was almost through, the stunt almost over. At the apex of her swing, Angela was supposed to simply let go of the rope and land lithely on the rock encrusted bank of the river. Shoulders burning with the strain, she almost could not wait. Her fingers, suddenly slick with her own blood, scrabbled to hang on the last few feet of the swing. Her heart was racing, her body cool and clammy in the spray of the falls. She counted- one... two ...

The rope snapped as Angela saw a shadow pass through her lifeline at blinding speed. It seemed an arrow, but Angela could not be sure as her attention had been focused on the small outcropping of rocks where she had been destined to land. She let out a scream of shock then, as she was suddenly flailing helplessly in the air, falling again.

She hit the water as she thought, slamming hard and sinking like a stone.

Karl Braun pushed off against the bank, using the oar as a pole to get his small boat moving across the writhing pool of water at the base of the falls. His heart was hammering in his chest, had been since he saw his girl suddenly tumble over the edge of the cliff high overhead. He watched helplessly as she fell, a feeling of dread coursing through his body as he watched Angela squirming in free fall, trying to salvage something from the stunt. Damn her, he thought, and damn to hell Gloria Swann as well.

Karl Braun had breathed a sigh of relief as he watched his girl swing up, up and away, then gasped as her line snapped and she was falling again, hitting the water as though dead.

Karl rowed for all he was worth, watching as Angela's helpless body swirled about and twisted beneath the churning waters of the raging pool beneath the falls. He had to reach her before she became trapped in the

"...she was suddenly...falling again."

grip of the current and was washed away further down the river towards the Amazon. She would be lost then, gone forever.

Angela sank, her head ringing from the impact of hitting the water. She had slammed into the pool flat on her back, the impact making her see stars and forcing the breath from her lungs as well. Her eyes were wide, stunned to see the churning water close above her, the dimming light of the setting sun quickly fading as she sank.

She started to gasp, to scream, and too late she realized what she was doing. Her lungs filled with water and she started to choke. Panic washed over her, as cold as the roiling pool that was sucking her down. She thrashed about; straining at the loose ropes still wrapped about her wrists, kicking at the unforgiving water. Her legs were lead, dragging her under. Spots danced before her eyes fading to gray.

A sudden jarring sparked her back to life, to awareness. She had hit the rocky bottom of the pool at the base of the falls and the pain in her own bottom had cleared her head somewhat. Still she gagged, struggling to get her bearings as she floated along, caught in the raging current. She twisted, her heart pounding in her ears, her lungs screaming to burst for air. Finding the riverbed again with her feet she pushed off, trying to pull off the trailing ropes as she kicked and paddled towards the surface. How far? Her sight was dimming. She could not see any light. Was she going the right direction?

Angela felt something snake down her back between her shirt and skin. If it was actually a snake, she was as good as dead. She had no fight left in her, no strength. She did not even gag as her shirt was hoisted up under her chin, constricting about her throat as the *something* jerked her up and out of the water. She felt a warm blast of dull, humid air as she gasped unable to catch her breath. Her chest was on fire. The world spinning out of control.

Her eyes popped open as awareness flooded back into her body. There was a face just inches away from her own, but it took a moment for her vision to focus and recognize the concerned visage of Karl Braun. Then her stomach heaved and she felt sour bile rising in her throat. She tried to cough but gagged instead, rolling onto her side with Karl's help as she hacked and vomited, spewing water from her lungs in a fit that would not seem to end.

Finally, her body heaving in agony with every breath Angela spat a final time and lay still. Her throat felt raw and ragged, and her stomach muscles were clenched in a tight knot that ached with the slightest movement. Her body felt like a sack of jelly as she rolled onto her back, looking up into the clear blue eyes of her stunt coordinator and friend. She tried to speak, but her throat clenched shut and she started to cough once more.

"Shhh…" Karl brushed her matted hair from her eyes and tried to make her settle down. "You rest. I'll get us back to shore." It was only then that Angela realized that they were still in Karl's small rowboat in the river. Her head was swimming and clogged, but she figured that Karl must have pulled her from the river and breathed some life back into her waterlogged body. Angela raised her arms as Karl began to row the boat back to the riverbank, all the while keeping one eye upon her. One bit of rope was still wrapped about one wrist, while the other bore the marks of her struggles. Red welts encircled both wrists, and her hands were skinned raw and still bleeding from sliding down the coarse rope in her fall. She could not feel the pain yet, it was just a dull, and far away ache numbed by the river, but she knew she would later. She struggled to sit up, but her head whirled, the dancing spots of gray blotting out her sight again. She felt a stab of pain as her head bounced off of the bottom of the boat. Then she felt nothing at all.

Angela sat in one of the fold up wood and canvas chairs scattered in haphazard fashion about the Make-up Tent. Her body ached all over, and she was trying her best to rest and recover as she leaned her head back over the large wash basin while the make-up girl, Carol Page, washed a colored rinse through her hair. It was a daily ritual that Angela had come to both dread and enjoy. It took almost an hour for the woman to get the tone of her hair just right, so that it matched the dye job of Gloria Swann, and Angela hated that hour of her life lost every day. She liked the attention though, as Carol always made her feel wonderful, massaging her scalp and making her feel more relaxed than any other time during her hectic schedule.

Angela Morgan sighed; fighting exhaustion as the woman ran her fingers through her hair. She remembered nothing after her brief encounter with Karl Braun in the boat, and had apparently slept through the entire night, awakening only to the gentle urgings of Carol trying to wake her for her morning make-up session. Her lungs still ached, as did her buttocks from bouncing off of the bottom of the river. Her hands hurt if she tried to make a fist, but that was almost impossible with the wrappings of bandages that the movie company's nurse had applied after Karl had gotten Angela out of the river. Her wrists were still pink and raw, but the swollen welts had already almost healed. Now she was just sore and tired, basically. She felt as though she could sleep a week if they would just let her.

Angela had moaned and protested when Carol had shaken her awake at the ungodly hour of four a.m. Someone had undressed her, getting her out of her water sodden clothes and into something loose and warm; a long woolen nightshirt, and put her to bed in her own cot in her tent. She suspected Karl, but had hoped it had been her friend, Jennifer Higgins or some of the other extras in the film. She had seen Jennifer still asleep on her own cot in the dim light of false dawn, wrapped in several thick blankets against the night's chill on the far side of the tent. Angela wondered how it could get so unbearably hot during the day and then be so freezing overnight that they all needed to be wrapped up against the cold. She had dressed quickly, suppressing the shivers, trying to be quiet until she heard the crack of thunder rolling in the distance. Seconds later it was pouring rain and she knew that it did not matter.

It was still pouring over an hour later as Carol wrung Angela's hair of excess water into the battered metal basin. Jennifer was sitting in the chair next to Angela, peering into the tall stand-up polished metal mirror propped against the wall of the tent as she poked and prodded a mosquito bite that had swelled on her shoulder over night. On her far side sat another of the Amazon extras, Martha Johnson, trying to sew up a snag that had appeared in her tiger skin costume. Both were busty young women, and were hired mainly for that reason for the movie. Both were pleasant though, and Angela enjoyed their company in their off hours.

"I thought Jonathan was gonna bust a gasket!" Martha continued, pausing only long enough to bite off the thread before going on about the day's gossip after Angela had passed out. "He was runnin' around like a chicken with his head cut off worryin' about you." Martha stood up and tugged at the hem of her skimpy costume, testing the strength of the stitching she had done.

"Really?" Angela said through gritted teeth as Carol gathered her hair tightly and squeezed with all her might.

"Oh, yeah!" Jennifer agreed, scratching at the bump on her arm with a grimace. "Karl was pushing on your belly and pumping your arms up and down and everybody else was near frantic with worry. He finally stopped when you spewed about a gallon of water out of your lungs. Jonathan finally calmed down after Karl said you'd be all right. Karl carried you all the way up the trail and to our tent, then me and Kathy got you undressed and dried before she bandaged your hands. Do they hurt much, Hon?"

"Not so much." Angela's voice quivered as Carol ruffled a towel through her hair. "I'm just lucky that the scheduled shots are off today 'cause of the rain." The company could do no outside filming with the pouring rain, so the director had decided to do close-ups until, if, the weather cleared. The way the rain was pounding on the tent though, Angela figured that it would be some time before the sky was clear again.

"It'll give me a chance to rest and heal up a bit." The other women nodded in agreement, Carol draping the damp, stained towel over the back of one of the empty chairs and taking a seat herself. From her make-up kit she pulled a pack of slim cigarettes and offered one to each of the other women. Jennifer declined, but the others lit up and before long all were laughing, relaxing, and trying to enjoy a rare, few free minutes.

It was awkward for Angela to hold her cigarette with her hands bandaged, but she did her best, trying to enjoy it, as she was able. Kathy Parker, the company nurse had done her usual bang-up job, cleaning and bandaging Angela's rope-burned hands. The nurse had given her a bit of morphine as well, for the pain and to help her sleep in some relative comfort. Angela was not as happy about that, as she had seen too many men come back from Europe at the end of the war addicted to drugs and painkillers. She did not want to go that route. A healthy swig of bourbon would have done just as well without the after effects.

"Gloria was livid," Martha continued, crushing the spent butt of her cigarette under the toe of her boot. "When Jonathan yelled 'cut' everyone ran up to the cliff to see if you were okay. Everyone 'cept her. The floozy bitch was still cursin' an' shoutin' at us, tryin' to find out who shot that last arrow."

"But nobody did!" Jennifer cut in. "At least, none of us did. You were lookin' right at us, Angela. We didn't do it!"

"I know…" Angela agreed, tossing the remains of her own cigarette to the dirt and crushing it out. "But somebody did. Somebody shot two arrows at me, into the dirt when I was at the cliff. That's why I fell. Remember?" Angela saw her friends nod, but none of them had any explanation. It was a real mystery, apparently, as the only bows and most of the arrows on the set were all accounted for, in the possession of the 'Amazons', all of whom were her friends. Sure, they might all like to turn Gloria Swann into a pincushion, but Angela did not think they felt that way about her as well.

She had not told anyone about the third arrow; the one that had severed the swing rope at a crucial moment, when she was swinging out over the river. She had not been sure, of course. She had been a bit preoccupied at the time, worrying about surviving the fall. And for an arrow to cut through the rope while it was moving! It seemed an impossible shot. If it had been an arrow, whoever had fired it would have had to have been a world class marksman. Or woman, she corrected. And the only person on the set that fit that bill was Gloria Swann herself, and she was accounted for. Besides, why would Gloria want her dead? It would ruin the movie, not to mention, well, killing her.

Angela rubbed at her temples, her mind swirling with too many questions. She was still exhausted, and suspected that the morphine was still making her sluggish and queer. She half expected to start shaking with the Screaming Meemies at any moment. She hated drugs!

"Angela…" She felt Jennifer's hand on her shoulder, warm and comforting. Angela looked up into Jennifer's big brown eyes and saw the concern in her face. "Are you all right?" Angela forced a smile.

"I'm fine. Just a little tired is all."

"Well, maybe we better…"

In almost theatrical fashion, lightning lit up the compound like the brightest day and thunder pealed immediately making all four women gasp and wince, yelping in surprise. Jennifer squeaked in shock as the tent flap flew open to reveal a shadowy figure silhouetted in the after glow of the lightning's flare. Rain was falling in sheets beyond the figure, as though the thunder had ripped a hole in the storm clouds above and all the stored water was suddenly falling in one fell swoop. The figure was dark and drenched, wearing a long rubber slicker with the hood pulled far over its head, shielding its face in the shadows and dripping water on the mat of weave carpeting by the tent's opening.

All four women were on their feet then, ready to run or defend themselves as the mysterious figure stepped into the tent, closing the flap behind. The figure bounced and shook, depositing still more water onto the muddy mat and dirt floor, then reached up and quickly flung back the concealing hood. A full mane of curly blonde hair seemed to explode from the hood as it was removed, and the four women gasped a collective sigh of relief as soon as they recognized that hair. There was only one woman on the set that had such an unruly mop of beautiful golden locks.

"What?"

Shirley Compton smiled innocently, giving the four women a curious glance as she fluffed her naturally curly hair back into shape and wiped a few stray strands from her face. The script girl was pretty, with a faint line of freckles dotting her nose and cheeks and a set of perfectly white teeth that produced a truly dazzling smile at her slightest whim. She had a perfect little body that almost every woman on the set was jealous of, and she seemed to be able to eat anything and everything without gaining an inch on her hourglass figure. Worse, she was nice, and she did not have the slightest clue as to how pretty she really was. Much as they tried to hate her, the other women just could not.

"What's wrong?" Shirley asked again, drawing a ribbon from her pocket and deftly snaring a handful of hair, tying it back into a big fluffy tail with a practiced ease. "Y'all look like ya saw a ghost."

Angela smiled, her heart still thumping in her chest like a native drum. Glancing at the others, she saw that they were just as jumpy as she was. She really wished that she had that bourbon.

"Sorry, Shirl. The storm's just got us all on edge I think."

"Oh, yeah." Shirley grinned, glancing back as another bolt of lightning lit the sky. "It's rainin' cats an' dogs out there. Isn't it great? Jus' like home." Shirley was from southern Georgia, if Angela recalled correctly, and in the South, they were used to sudden sultry storms springing up at the drop of a hat. Only she would think it was great.

"What's the deal, Shirl?" Martha asked, though already knowing the answer, apparently, as she began stuffing her things into her carryall bag. Carol too was packing up, replacing her make-up in their proper kits and putting each back into her case. They all knew that when Shirley came around it usually meant business.

"Jonathan wants the Amazons in the Production Tent for close-ups. Sorry gals."

Martha shrugged. "Hey, that's what we're here for, right?"

Shirley waited as the three women gathered their belongings and pulled their own slickers over head preparing to brave the storm. She glanced at Angela, flashing her a wide, toothy smile. "Feelin' better?"

"A little." Angela smiled back and held up her bandaged hands. "It'll be a day or two yet, I think. Lucky for me it's raining."

"Yeah…" Shirley smiled again, then looked away, replacing her hood as she stepped back to the tent flap. "Ready?" she asked the other three, but before they could answer she was already out of the tent and dashing across the compound. With a shrug and hasty goodbye to Angela, Martha and Carol ran out as well, hot on the script girl's heels, nimbly trying to dodge the deeper pools of water that were forming along the beaten path. Jennifer paused at the tent flap and looked back at her friend with some concern. Her eyes were sparkling eerily in the deep shadows of the slicker's hood.

"Are you going to be all right?" she asked, staring at Angela.

Angela Morgan smiled and nodded. "I'll be fine, Jenn. Go!"

She saw Jennifer smirk. "Okay. But you try to get some rest. That's an order!"

"Yes, ma'am." Angela saluted, then stood as her friend dashed out into the pouring rain. She secured the flap with a twist of cotton cord then settled down on her cot to relax. She wanted to sleep, but her head was still swimming with questions over the arrows and who might have fired them. She ran a list of everyone on the set, but all were accounted for at the time, if not directly involved with the shot, then on the fringes watching. The filming of the stunts was always a long and tedious affair to set up, but watching the stunt in action was always thrilling and no one ever missed one.

Angela ran a hand through her hair and found that it was still damp, so she could not lie down anyway. She might get sick with a wet head, or worse, she might wake up with a flat spot in her hair. She would then have to have Carol start all over again and listen to a speech while she was trying to set things right. Angela could do without a speech.

Finally, Angela settled into one of the canvas chairs, propped her feet up on another and draped a thick blanket over her legs against the chills. She picked up her script and started to read, thumbing through the notes Karl had added concerning her next stunt. It had not started out to be a stunt, but as soon as Jonathan had seen the rapids just a ways downstream from the falls it had quickly grown into one. A simple shot of Gloria running along the riverbank had turned into Angela struggling against the current of the river as it carried her downstream after she had fallen into the water. Jonathan had scribbled in his corrections, which Shirley had then copied and delivered to everyone who would be involved. Karl had mapped out the stunt, so Angela was relatively certain that it was safe, but she still had her reservations.

Angela hated to swim.

Angela Morgan fidgeted only a little as Karl Braun loosely wrapped the slim leather cord about her wrists. It was not tight, and barely knotted, but there was less play between her wrists than she would have liked. She glanced at the rain-swollen river rushing past just a few feet away, the white water churning and spewing spray as it crashed over rocks submerged in its depths. She shivered, then swallowed. She was not looking forward to this. She hated swimming, but in the scene she figured she would be doing little of that.

"Nervous?"

Angela looked up as Karl knotted off the last of the cord and gave her a reassuring smile. Angela tried to smile back, but her heart just was not in it. She shivered again, telling herself it was just the chill of the morning air.

It was two days, almost, since the storm had first begun and there were still lingering clouds that occasionally spat out a drizzle of rain. A cool wind was blowing in the storm's wake, and almost everyone was wearing a light jacket of some sort, or at least their rain ponchos for their meager protection. Everyone but Angela, that is, as she was in the next shot, and she had not been wearing a coat when she had made her leap from the cliff. Still, despite the sprinkles, and the chill, it was turning into a beautiful day. The sun was huge in the east, just a little ways over the horizon, and the air after the storm was crisp and fresh. Angela knew that it would not be long before the humidity settled in again, so she was determined to enjoy it while she could.

Karl grabbed her hands then, still talking. "You should not be worried, liebchen. It is a simple task. One you could do with your hands tied behind your back, yes?" He chuckled, turning her hands over as far as the cord would allow, inspecting the ropes a final time as well as the gloves she was wearing. He had insisted that she wear the gloves; a pair of calf leather that were soft and as close to the color of her skin that they could find. Angela smirked. They were Gloria's, and probably expensive. She wondered if the movie star even knew that they were missing.

Kathy had rewrapped her bandages that morning, cleaning the wounds again in the process. Two days later, they were not as deep as they had first appeared, but they still hurt a bit. There were raw pink stripes on both of Angela's hands where her skin had ripped away but Kathy Parker the nurse had said that they were healing nicely. With the smaller bandages in place, Karl had then slipped the gloves onto her hands and sealed them on with a bit of surgical bandage wrapped about each wrist which was in turn hidden by the binding cord. He assured her that it would be water proof, at least for awhile, and that would help once she got into the chilly river.

Angela pulled against the leather cords at Karl's direction, making sure that the bindings were tight enough to stay in place but not so loose that they might slip away and spoil the shot. They appeared fine, to both of their satisfactions, so Karl led Angela down the slight trail to the water's edge talking all the way.

"There will be a camera there…and there." He pointed and Angela looked up to the cliff's edge where she had jumped a little over two days before. She saw the camera perched on the ledge with several of the crew gathered around to watch. Jonathan Harkins was there, and Gloria as well as Shirley and some of the others that never strayed too far from the director's side. A whole crowd in fact, watching from the relative safety of the cliff so as to stay out of the way. Angela almost wished that she were up there with them, watching as someone else, Gloria in fact, as she had to brave the rapids.

Angela's gaze followed where Karl was pointing and she spied the second camera set up across the river on a small outcropping of rock. Jimmy Barton, the young operator was busy wiping down the lens as one of the film handlers sorted spools nearby. Jimmy was barely eighteen, but he was a well-respected operator and had been in the business for most of his life. He was a 'studio brat'; his mother a character extra and her father a gaffer. Jimmy had been a gopher when Angela had been cast in her first role as Gloria's stand-in. He waved when he saw her looking, doffing his cap with a flourish and a smile.

"The third camera's about a quarter mile down river. That's where I'll be, waiting to pull you out if anything goes wrong. Katherine will be there too. Not a worry, eh?"

"Easy for you to say," Angela quipped as she stepped into the shallows along the riverbank. Karl steadied her until she found her footing, then stepped away as Angela squatted down into the chilly water until it was up to her neck. She moaned, cursing under her breath as the water passed over her nipples. "It's freezing!" she snarled, her teeth already chattering, but Karl simply chuckled.

"That is why you make the big money." Angela glared evilly as Karl backed away up the riverbank. He paused at the trail, watching as she eased out of the calm along the river's edge and towards the swifter current that would carry her towards the rapids. "Remember to try not to fight the river. Let it carry you, and take the rapids feet first. Your head is strong and hard, but not that much, I think." Karl rapped his knuckles against the side of his head with a grin, then jogged down the path and out of sight.

Angela was alone. With a final sigh she gritted her teeth and steeled herself against the chill of the river, then moved even further out into the stream. She felt the current tugging at her, sweeping her skirt about her legs. The rocks underfoot were slick with moss and worn from year upon year of the rushing water. Angela looped her arms about a stone jutting from the surface about a quarter of the way across the water and let the current turn her about until she was facing the cliff and the falls in the distance. When she was satisfied with her position and found her footing she glanced over at Jimmy and nodded. Jimmy in turn waved up at the crew on the cliff.

Angela watched as Jonathan Harkins started giving orders, readying everyone into position for the shot. It was almost laughable how everyone suddenly seemed to scurry about at his command, hurrying off to do whatever job they had to do. Everyone but Gloria. The 'Wicked Witch of East Hollywood' simply stared that cold stare of hers, waiting for Angela to make her look good once again.

Angela tensed as Jonathan raised his megaphone to his lips, his free arm stretched overhead so that all could see. She could not hear him yet, but she could imagine what he was saying: "Ready! Camera! ..." She saw Jimmy from the corner of her eye, training his camera on her, the handler watching the cliff with a hand resting on Jimmy's shoulder ready to give the word to 'roll film'. She wondered if Karl was in place downstream yet.

Angela pushed off into the current as Jonathan Harkins slashed his arm through the air. She could not hear his voice over the roar of the falls, but he had given the signal, and Angela started counting, kicking her legs as she made her way towards the rapids. At the count of five she knew that the cliff camera would start to film, and she would have to be in the current by then, for the best shot. By ten she would be passing Jimmy, and struggling frantically, or so it would appear to his camera, fighting for her life as she was swept down the river.

She felt the strength of the river almost instantly as it scooped her up in its grip and started to carry her along. It was swifter than she thought it would be raging harder from the rain, and Angela was hard pressed simply to keep her head above water let alone keep on course. She tried her best to keep her feet out in front of her, letting her legs absorb the brunt of the fast paced impacts as she tumbled along from rock to rock. She was glad now that the submerged stones were worn and slick with age and moss, as had they been rough, her legs and buttocks would already be ripped to shreds.

She scrambled along, more running along the bottom of the river than swimming. Her legs were churning slowly but furiously against the river's flow as she tried to stay upright and above the water, trying to stay in view of the cameras. Jonathan had told her to thrash about as much as possible as she swam downriver, to 'play up her distress', caught in the grip of the current, and she was finding that far easier to do than she would have hoped. The river threw her about with ease, despite her best efforts, slamming her from rock to rock, twisting her body and even tossing Angela into the air at times. It was hard to breathe as well. It seemed that whenever she opened her mouth to gasp for breath, the river would twist her about, shoving her face into the drink making her gulp water instead of air. Angela was coughing and spluttering before long, and suddenly worried.

She saw up ahead a small drop in the river's course; a fall of maybe ten feet. Karl had inspected the entire length of the run yesterday and had told her about the upcoming waterfall, and what dangers awaited her there. A short drop into a deep pool with only a few rocks to worry about during the plunge. Angela tried to veer towards her left as he had suggested in order to hit the pool beyond and below at the best spot to avoid the stones. She also struggled to get upright again, in order to go over the falls feet first, just in case. It would not do to sprawl over the drop headfirst, to be smashed against an errant rock or to be sucked down into the churning undertow below the falls. Angela thrashed about, as she had been told, all the while thrusting up and out of the water to gulp down great lung fulls of air when she could. She played for the cameras, knowing that within moments she would be out of their sight for a bit; a few seconds actually, until she was picked up by the third camera further down the river where Karl and Kathy waited with John Thomas, the Assistant Director and the rest of the site crew.

Suddenly she was falling. Angela stared wide-eyed as the world spun about overhead, a bright blue sky dotted with clouds framing a golden sun. The surrounding jungle seemed topsy-turvy for a long, frozen heartbeat. Her ears filled with the rushing, crashing roar of water. She gasped as pain shot though her neck.

Angela splashed down into the pool of frothing white foam, immediately sinking, being sucked down into the churning darkness by the pressure of the falling water. Her body was tossed about like a rag-doll as she frantically kicked her legs, trying to reach the surface again. She was exhausted from fighting the river already, and her long skirt and waterlogged clothes hindered her movements and threatened to drag her down. The pool was far deeper than she thought it might be, and she was disoriented as she struggled, seeing the sparkling glow of the sun overhead, rippling through the depths. Her neck and shoulder stung with pain, stiffening as she doubled her efforts, though she had thought that she had hit the water on her hip and side more than her shoulders. It hurt to move, her legs feeling leaden and rubbery all at once. She was seeing gray, little spots exploding before her eyes as her lungs threatened to explode. So soon.

Too soon… Where was the surface?

Angela felt something slam against her back, and involuntarily felt the last of her waning air forced from her lungs. Water filled her mouth, pushing down her throat to fill the sudden void. Angela struggled to right herself, to get her bearings as the gray crowded closer from the edges of her sight. She spun around, something smashing against her temple, then scraping along her leg. The world was spinning out of control. Getting darker.

Darker…

EPISODE THREE:
THE RIVER OF NO RETURN!

*A*ngela gasped, filling her lungs with air as she broke surface again. She had felt something sting her neck, just before she hit the water but paid it no heed at the moment though it seemed to almost burn in the air. She had more important worries to concern her as the icy grip of the river took hold and dragged her down into the dark, writhing depths again.

El Gato Negra waited, crouching in the cool damp darkness in the hollow of the stone alcove behind the waterfall. She had been there for hours, settling in, in the darkness of night, waiting for her brief moment, when the time would be ripe to strike. She had waited, silently, watching as the darkness thinned, the black fading to purple then gray and the first rays of the glorious sun shown down, her mind intent, focused on the hunt. The kill.

The warmth of the sun did not reach the hollow of the cave behind the falls, and the light, though sparkling and bright, did little to illuminate her hidden lair. El Gato Negra did not care. Like the great black leopard that was her namesake, her avatar, she preferred the quiet still of the night, and she had spent many times far longer waiting, unmoving for hours in the trees or brush, awaiting her unwary prey.

She had espied the hole the day before as she had been pacing the older *Blanca* as he himself had paced the stream. He had been following the course, making note of rocks and calms, mapping the waters along a short distance from the rocky bank, looking for danger. So intent on his mission was he, that he did not even realize that he was in turn being watched and followed so closely. He was oblivious to all about him, ignorant of the jungle and its inhabitants. That would be his downfall, his death, she thought. One must ever be aware of the *Green*, lest it swallow one whole.

The whites were all ignorant of the Green. The rain forest was a fast friend to those that knew *Her* ways, granting life to those *She* found worthy. She was also a harsh mistress to those She found wanting, fools like these outlanders that had come stumbling into Her rich embrace, hacking and cutting away at Her flesh, burning Her with their fires and choking Her children with their foulness. They were a blight on the land, a plague to be vanquished lest their carrion touch forever taint the forest, the jungle, home.

As Priestess of the People, it fell to her to rid the land of these foul, fool invaders. It would be a simple matter, of course, as they were like children, stumbling blindly, naively onward, and ever closer to their doom. Still, Selia, El Gato Negra, High Priestess of the Cult of the Jaguar, Defenders of the Green and all Her children was not ignorant of the ways of the world beyond her own lands. She knew that if she did not use her guile and cunning, if she scared the outlanders away with a show of force rather than well disguised trickery, then they would be back in greater numbers, with more odd machines and their guns. She could not just kill them all outright, though she knew that her sisters could easily slay them all, and wanted to. If the outlanders simply vanished, Selia knew that others would come to investigate, however, so she needed to drive them out with a fear of the Green embedded in their hearts.

Selia had tainted their foods with sickness that first night, easily stealing into their camp and lacing their stores and water with the *Breath of the Viper*. The whites had something though, herbs and potions of their own to ease the sickness and they remained, ill but determined. She had damaged their machines next, smashing those things that she could as an animal might; ripping through their thick-skinned tents and scattering the strange metal wheels of stiff, shining skin that they savored. This had angered them, and Selia watched horrified as the men of their group stormed through the jungles, slaying anything that they saw with their

*"…lacing their …water with the **Breath of the Viper**."*

deafening thunder-sticks, their guns. Now they guarded their camp at night, firing blindly at any noise or movement in the darkness. That had been a mistake on her part, and one she would not make again. She would not again underestimate the determination of the outlanders.

Taking a more direct approach, Selia had watched, following the group through their strange daily rituals. She had found it odd when a trio of their women, dressed in garb not unlike her own animal skins and leathers, began to chase a fourth older woman through the jungle while the others watched. The trio fired arrows at their 'friend', though none came near enough to harm her. It was then that Selia formed a daring plan. She ran ahead, seeing where the trio of 'warriors' were herding the fourth, and concealed herself in the trees, waiting for her opportunity to strike. As the older woman edged closer to the cliff over the falls, Selia had joined in the firing of arrows, aiming not to kill, but to force the woman over the edge of the cliff. It had almost worked.

She had tried again, when a younger version of the woman had replaced the elder, much to Selia's bewilderment. Their customs were so strange. There was much shouting as the women traded places at the precipice, but Selia waited, taking aim until all were focused on their strange tasks. El Gato Negra's aim was true, and her arrows caused the younger woman to fall from the ledge, but she was a lucky one, even blessed perhaps. The woman, even bound at the wrists in some bizarre ritual of the outlanders had managed to grab a low hanging vine and swing safely from her plunge. Selia had severed the vine with another arrow, but to no avail. The woman hit the water like a stone, but her fellows, the older Blanca, had fished her out and rescued her from the river's clutches before she could be swept away and drown.

So Selia waited.

The rains had come, and the whites were stalled, huddling together during the storm that raged for two whole days. Selia had watched, however, stealing into their camp and listening, learning their movements and traditions, trying to fathom what they were about. She was used to the rains, and the pounding force from the heavens did not deter her from her path, her duty.

And now her time had come again. She watched the water falling in a sheet before the mouth of the hollow where she hid. She crouched, waiting; the long hollow tube of dried reed gingerly touching her lips. She would have less than a heartbeat to draw breath and fire with enough force to pierce the cascade of falling water and the skin of the younger woman as well, but Selia was confident. She was one with the Green, and the Goddess would guide her, making her aim true.

A shadow appeared and Selia drew breath, blowing through the hollow tube at once. She saw the flash of the dart as it whisked through the air, disappearing into the wall of water. She was certain that her aim was sure as the shadow of the woman fell past the opening of her cave to splash into the pool below a moment later. She was sure that the dart had struck its mark, the poisons coating the tip already working their magic on the woman; making her groggy and weak, stiffening her limbs, easing into her life's blood and flowing towards her heart. She would soon be dead, and the outlanders would panic, their devious plans disrupted. Disheartened at the death of one of their own, they would leave, never to return. Of that Selia was certain.

"*Engel...*"

Karl Braun felt his heart skip a beat as he watched his girl plummet over the falls. Despite his warnings Angela had hit the falls wrong, falling over the edge awkwardly, almost head first. She was hurt, he was sure, as he saw her body jerk just before hitting the water, disappearing beneath the churning cauldron below the falls. And now...

Now she had not come up again.

Karl Braun started forward, determined to wade into the river and drag his girl out. Something was most definitely wrong. Panic swelled within him as he began to shout her name.

"Hold on there, Karl."

The aging stunt master felt a hand fall on his shoulder, holding him back. Disbelief in his eyes, he turned to see the Assistant Director holding him in place. John Thomas was staring intently at the river, anticipation and excitement holding his own attention barely in check. He licked his lips, the slight breeze fluttering the red kerchief tied loosely about his neck.

"Let's give her a minute, see what happens."

Karl shrugged the hand from his shoulder and turned away, ignoring the suggestions of his superior. In the Hollywood pecking order, though a stunt coordinator was important, a director ruled. Braun felt the hand again as he started forward; more forceful than before as it grabbed his arm tightly and spun him around.

"I said wait, Braun! This is great stuff!" A smug smile twisted Thomas' lips as Karl Braun stared in disbelief.

"But..." he stammered, "Angela is..."

"Angela is a grown woman and she can take care of herself. Look!"

Karl turned back, watching breathlessly as Angela's head broke the surface of the river. She was coughing, spitting up water, but her arms were flailing as she tried to swim, fighting the strong current. Still, she seemed dazed, her face twisted in pain and her movements sluggish and strained. She had freed herself from the ropes, the bindings still trailing from her wrists as they were supposed to, playing for drama for the camera. She was struggling with every stroke however, and it was killing Karl Braun to stand helplessly and wait.

Thomas still held him back, the director's eyes focused on the scene as he gave orders to the crew scrambling about him. Joey Hunt was busily cranking away at his camera, his own expression unreadable as he leaned into the viewfinder. Jackson Walters, one of the film's editors stood with a look of glee on his face, his body almost shaking with excitement. Only Katherine Parker seemed to share Karl's distress and worry over the girl in danger, but she made no move to help, held in check by Thomas as was he.

As Karl Braun turned back once again, he saw that Angela Morgan had fought her way closer to the shore. She was trying to stand in the torrent, her face pleading for help, though no cry escaped her lips. She looked haggard and worn, and drenched of course, from her wild ride in the river. Karl pulled on Thomas' grip, wanting to charge to her rescue, but the director held him firm.

"Hold on… Just a little more… Cut! Print!"

Karl surged forward, Kathy Parker hot on his heels just as Angela staggered into the calmer shallows at the edge of the river. Together they splashed into the water as Angela moaned and swooned, collapsing into the stunt coordinator's waiting arms. Karl gasped, feeling the icy touch of her skin, but Kathy was at his side and already administering to the ailing young woman.

"Get her to the bank!" the nurse commanded, and Karl scooped his girl up into his arms without question or protest, splashing back to the shore immediately. Once there, he laid Angela flat as Kathy dropped to her knees beside the stunt girl and tried to force the water from her lungs. The nurse pumped Angela's arms up and down, and her legs as well, and finally leaned in, kissing the younger woman, or so it appeared. Karl watched, panic rising within him again as the nurse repeated the odd process, wanting to help, wanting to take over and feeling useless. If Angela died, he would die as well, never able to forgive himself.

Karl gasped as he heard Angela choke, spewing water from her lungs then hacking and coughing. Kathy leaned back, her own face wet and streaked with concern as their friend rolled onto her side and vomited seeming gallons of water. Braun glanced at the rest of the crew, but they were only half watching as they secured the fresh roll of film that they had just shot. Karl cursed under his breath at their callousness, and his own for letting Thomas hold him back.

"Gawd…"

Karl crouched down beside his girl, Kathy still kneeling across as Angela tried to sit up. She was soaked to the bone, but seemed to be sweating and shivering all at once. Goose bumps ran rampant along her exposed arms and legs, and she seemed weak, as though her limbs had grown numb and fallen asleep. Kathy Parker the nurse was patting her friend on the back, trying to get her to cough up the remainder of the water she had swallowed.

"Engel? Are you all right?" Karl asked frantically, his voice croaking with concern.

Angela coughed, but tried to force a smile as she glanced blearily at her boss. Karl relaxed when he saw the weak effort, and he knew that she would survive…again. "What happened?"

"I…I dunno…" Angela gasped, hacking again. "I was…trying to do what you said… But I guess I hit the falls wrong. Fell and couldn't get right… I'm sorry…"

Karl Braun brushed the girl's hair from her face, forcing himself to smile, for her sake. His opinion mattered to her, and he knew that she cared what he thought, that her every stunt was an effort to make him proud. And he was. He swelled with pride every time she finished one of his stunts successfully. He was so thankful each time she survived, knowing that every stunt and situation that he thought up and put her in was more dangerous than the last. Still, Karl Braun knew that she would survive, and accomplish the stunt far better than he might ever have imagined. Angela Morgan was a natural, the best stunt person that he had ever worked with and gifted beyond belief. He was so proud that she thought so highly of him, and his work. Angela was like a daughter to him, or the son he never had. She was his protégé and successor, heir to his knowledge and abilities.

"It is all right." He rubbed her back, assuring her that she had done fine as Katherine the nurse ran her own hands lightly over Angela's body to make sure that there were no injuries that were not blatantly evident. Karl watched, shushing Angela's protests until Kathy nodded her approval. He saw the nurse' fist curl about something but paid it no mind as he scooped the girl up into his arms once more.

"Hey!" Angela protested for only a moment, until fatigue drained all the strength from her struggles once again, her adrenaline rush fading and nausea settling in after the adventure. Karl shrugged her light form into a comfortable cradle, then stood easily supporting her weight.

"Quiet!" he ordered with a friendly smile. "You are in no shape to walk back to camp. With the Director's permission, I will carry you there, if he is done with you." Karl turned towards Thomas who was supervising the transfer of the camera into a protective metal canister. The Assistant Director said nothing, so intent on his task, but waved the trio away. A blessing of sorts, and Karl took advantage and started towards the path back to the camp over a mile away. Angela settled into his arms, already nodding with exhaustion and secure, knowing that protest would be useless.

"Home, James…" She smiled, and Karl Braun chuckled as she drifted off to sleep in his arms.

"What is that?"

Jennifer Higgins leaned forward, staring at the small, feathered thing held gingerly in the fingers of Kathy Parker, the nurse. It looked like a 'fly' a fishhook decked out in feathers and fuzzy bits of material, except that the hook was straight and pointed. She had seen enough flies growing up along the Missouri River to note the resemblance. Her father had been an addict, up at the crack of dawn and away for hours, sometimes days at a time, coming home again smelling and filthy but without a single fish for his efforts. He loved the sport, as he called it since the family did not need the meat despite the hard times of the Depression. Jennifer never saw the attraction, however, despite the hours she spent at his side, shivering in the cold, sweltering in the heat, getting drenched in the pouring rain, pole in hand and line in the river.

"It's a dart, I think." Kathy Parker turned the feathered dart about in her fingers to give the young woman a thorough look. It was barely half an inch long, fletched with small, soggy feathers and a short, sharp obsidian needle at one end. "I found it in Angela's neck. It barely broke the skin, but I think this is what caused her to weaken and stiffen up in that last stunt." Kathy took a long, final drag off of her cigarette then dropped it to the dirt floor of her First Aid Tent, grinding the butt out beneath the heel of her boot.

"How so?" Jennifer asked, staring at the dart but not comprehending how something so small could have caused so much trouble.

"I think it might have been coated with some type of poison. Curare maybe, or something else more locally exotic. I'm not sure."

"Really?" Jennifer gasped, staring harder at the little dart. She had heard of Curare, a foul drug used by the South American natives, though she did not really know exactly what it did.

"Angela said that she felt stiff in the limbs, and numb. Curare paralyzes the victim, eventually causing heart failure, among other things. I think that Angela would be dead right now, except that this dart was not coated well enough, or maybe the water washed away most of the poison. Maybe the dart didn't go into her deeply enough." Kathy shrugged, dropping the dart into a small metal box and putting that into one of her carry-bags. "I don't know. It's beyond what I learned in school. All's I do know is that somebody tried to off our girl, Angela."

"But who?" Jennifer held her palms up, scrunching her shoulders to show her confusion. "Who would want Angela dead?"

"I don't know." Kathy sighed, lighting another cigarette and settling back into her fold-up canvas chair. She propped her feet up on the small table that held some of her medicines and tools of her trade, crossing her legs at the ankles as she tried to think. "Maybe the local natives aren't as friendly as they seem. Or, maybe somebody in our little group wants us to think that. Whatever, you better spread the word to keep an eye out. Don't tell Karl or Angela, and for God's sake don't tell the two Johnnies or Miss High and Mighty Swann. Let's just keep this at our level for now, and see what else happens."

"Sure, Kathy. Whatever you say." Jennifer Higgins smiled weakly, staring out at the compound through the mosquito mesh that covered the opening at the flap of the tent. They were already setting up for the next major scene, and she would be needed all too soon, but her mind was not into the task at hand any more. Someone was trying to kill Angela, maybe all of them as she remembered the bout of sickness that they all experienced those first few nights. Kathy had said that it was the local water, and that had seemed reasonable, but then there was the animal that had attacked the camp one night, destroying critical footage and equipment in a not so haphazard manner now that she thought about it. And what about the arrows?

Jennifer stood, straightening her skimpy costume of torn leather and animal skin. She jiggled her bosom back into place as Shirley the script girl jogged past calling out for the 'Amazons' to come to the set. Time to get back to work.

"Not so damn ti...mmmph!"

Gloria Swann cursed under her breath, fuming as the three women held her to the ground and tied her up. They seemed to be enjoying themselves, the three bit players dressed as Amazon warrior women; one straddling her stomach and tying her wrists together, another binding her ankles as she kicked for the camera, struggling to get away. The third, Jennifer she thought, was kneeling near her head and had clamped her hands over her mouth, effectively stifling Gloria's protests. Gloria winced as the thin leather bindings were cinched tightly, biting into her wrists.

She hated this part of her job. She was above the physical activities involved in a shoot, had been for years. She hated the running, and the exertion, the struggles. She knew of course that she must be authentic, that she must be in some of the scenes or her fans might realize that she was using a stunt stand in. But, dammit, that was what that little snot Angela was being paid for. She was the one that should be running through the hot, filthy jungle. She was the one that should have been tackled into the mud, wrestled and bound like a pig for the slaughter. Gloria Swann had paid her dues, after all, and was beyond such things. She was an Actor!

That big-tittied cow, Martha knotted off the cord that she had been wrapping about Gloria's wrists and nodded to Jennifer. The younger woman smiled, producing a strip of animal skin that she snapped tight and forced between Gloria's lips, then knotted behind her head. Gloria grunted at the fierceness of the bindings; the gag biting into her face, pinching her cheeks together, the leather cords about her wrists so tight that her fingers were tingling as blood drained away. Even the ropes about her ankles were overly tight, causing her feet to hurt and restricting her movement beyond imagination.

On cue the three women stood, stepping away as the camera was repositioned to get a better, close-up view of Gloria as she writhed and struggled in her bonds on the damp and muddy jungle floor. Gloria was filthy, and she hated it. She was hot and perspiring, as the weather had grown humid over night, and she hated that more. And, she was not in control. She hated that most of all.

Still, she was an actress; the *best* actress, and she would survive. She stared pleadingly up into the eye of the camera as she fought against her tight bindings. She could see that little brat, Jimmy Barton, licking his lips with lust as he steadied the camera on her helpless form. He was enjoying the way that she struggled, pulling against her bindings and writhing about on the ground. He was the perfect example of one of her fans, and watching his reaction, Gloria knew what her followers wanted. She knew that she was a great actress; the greatest. But she also knew that it was pimply-faced perverts like Jimmy that kept her on top of her game and made her *Numero Uno* at the box-office.

Gloria gasped, screaming into her gag as Amazon Number One appeared with a stout wooden pole about six feet long. For a moment terror wracked her body and she struggled all the harder. In her mind's eye, she imagined the worst. Then, the woman, Alice something, slid the rod under her bindings at ankle and wrist, then hefted her up and into the air with the help of Martha the cow. Gloria grunted in pain as the women bounced her into a comfortable position, adjusting her weight for their comfort but ignoring her own as all of her pounds settled onto her bound wrists and ankles, straining her limbs and the wooden pole alike.

Gloria Swann craned her neck, straining to see Harkins, waiting as patiently as she could for the bastard to yell cut and end her torment. She focused on him finally, sitting off to the side as he glanced at the script that Shirley held for him, nodding silently as she pointed at something. He was smiling, ignoring her, and that made Gloria fume all the more. She shook and fought, pulling on the cords that held her bound, dangling from the pole that she was suspended from as her captors giggled and jogged off down the jungle path, the camera no doubt focusing on their bouncing butts rather than Gloria's authentic facial expressions.

Gloria screamed!

Gloria grunted as Martha and Alice deposited her none too gently onto the jungle path. She was breathing hard through her nose, and sweating like a pig in the humidity. It seemed the further they all went into the jungle, the hotter it got, and Gloria could see that her three 'captors' were glistening with sweat as well. Jennifer Higgins, the third of the three Amazons plopped onto a small rock and stared down at Gloria, wiping the sweat from her brow with a handkerchief that she had stuffed down into her brassiere.

"Christ Almighty. How far do we have to carry her?" she wheezed, sounding as out of breath as Gloria was from her screaming. "Did anyone hear Jonathan call 'cut'?" Gloria watched as the two other scantily clad women shrugged, shaking their heads. Gloria had her doubts that the camera could even see them anymore and felt that she should be untied. The shot was over, obviously, and she was parched. Gloria Swann moaned into her gag, but the leather skin stuffing her mouth was dry and constricting so that her protestations came out as muffled grunts. Still, Jennifer glanced her way.

"Maybe we should untie her."

"Better not," Martha said, leaning against a rock of her own. "Jonathan'll be pissed if we undo the knots and he has to redo the shot. It won't be perfect, and I'm sure that Gloria, Miss Swann wants her movie to be perfect." Martha stared at Gloria's helpless form and nudged her with the toe of her tiger skin boot, a wide smile curling her lips. "Isn't that right, Miss Swann?"

Gloria grunted and struggled at her bonds. The woman was right, damn her eyes, but not to the extent that Gloria Swann should be treated so. Gloria fumed, staring daggers at the grinning Martha Johnson, swearing that she would see the bitch burn in hell.

Minutes ticked by as the three Amazons watched with some amusement as Gloria rolled about on the dirty jungle trail, trying to get free. Gloria Swann was soon whimpering with frustration, wondering why she could not escape. Once upon a time she had been the greatest escape artist alive, but now she could not even get out of the simple bindings at her wrists and ankles. Worse, every time she reached up to at least undo her tight, stifling gag, one of her three captors would stop her. She was the 'Queen of Escapes' for God's sake, but she was helpless.

Finally, bored and tired of watching Gloria's escape attempts, Jennifer glanced at her friends. "Maybe one of us should go back and see what's up? The others should have been here by now with the camera, don't you think?"

Alice and Martha were instantly on their feet. "We'll go, Jenny. You stay here and watch out for her." Martha pointed at the helpless Gloria. "Make sure she doesn't get loose so we have to do this all over again." And before Jennifer or Gloria could protest, the two women were jogging back the way they had come, soon to disappear into the thick foliage. Jennifer turned back to Gloria and shrugged, smiling weakly.

"Sorry." She forced a smile, then adjusted her rump on the rock, trying to get comfortable, not knowing how long they might have to wait.

Gloria stared at the amply endowed young woman, trying her best to burn a hole through her body with her fiercest gaze. The girl was ignoring Gloria's moans of pain, leaning back with her eyes closed as she tried to absorb the warming rays of the sun. Gloria cursed, snarling into her gag to be freed, but after a brief glance to make sure that nothing was wrong, the girl ignored her. Mentally Gloria counted the tortures that she would inflict on the little bitch.

Gloria screamed into her gag with all of her might as the jungle greenery parted behind the reclining Jennifer Higgins. Her eyes widened in shock and sudden fear as three women; three different women stepped silently from the bushes. Gloria gasped, trying to scream a warning to the bit extra as one of the new women raised an evil, heavy looking stick over Jennifer and brought it down upon her head. There was a sickening thud, and Jennifer moaned, then slid to the ground beside Gloria in a senseless heap.

The Queen of Escapes stared up at the three women, absolute terror gripping her. She struggled mightily at her bonds, fearing for her life as the trio stepped forward, towering over her helpless form. They were dressed almost exactly like the extras from the movie; wearing beaten animal skins that barely covered their taut bodies and held their ample breasts in check. They were all dark-skinned, Indians native to South America, though far taller than any normal people that she had seen over the past few weeks. All were at least six feet tall, with long flowing hair as dark as night and slim, dusky bodies in perfect shape. They were remarkably beautiful, and Gloria, despite her predicament, suddenly felt very self-conscious.

One dressed in jet-black furs, golden bangles and darker and more beautiful than the others stepped up by Gloria's head and squatted down beside her. She grabbed Gloria's chin despite her muffled grunts of protest, turning the star's head back and forth as though examining her. Gloria half-expected the woman to rip off her gag and check her teeth for cavities. Images of a huge black cooking pot danced through Gloria's imagination, and she sincerely hoped that she was not being considered for the main course of the trio's next meal.

Gloria wrinkled her nose in disgust as the rough, dirty hands patted her cheek playfully. The woman in the black furs said something in some guttural native language that caused her companions to laugh, then she stood up. The two other women strode forward, and for the first time Gloria noticed that both wore long knives strapped to their thighs. The terror returned, redoubled as they reached for her.

Gloria grunted in pain as the two Amazons hefted her easily to their shoulders, suspending her from the pole again that the actresses had been carrying her with not so long before. The dark clad woman barked some command after the two had settled her weight, and suddenly both broke into a swift trot through the jungle, following some path that Gloria could not see.

Pain shot through Gloria's wrists and ankles as her own weight started to wear on her limbs from the jostling. Her arms and legs ached, and her throat was parched and dry as a desert. Worse, the swift pace that the two women set had her bouncing in her bonds and every step seemed to put an even greater strain on her legs and shoulders. It was not long before Gloria was moaning in agony and tears were flowing freely down her face. She was being kidnapped. Tortured!

And there was not a blessed thing that Gloria Swann could do about it, save scream.

❀   ❀   ❀

EPISODE FOUR:
PRISONER OF THE AMAZONS!

*G*loria Swann struggled desperately as the three women bound her to the pole.

It seemed like hours since she had first been lashed to the carry-pole by the three extras from the film, the 'Amazon women,' and carried into the jungle like a deer carcass. In actuality, it had only been minutes. It had all been a part of the movie that they were shooting in the jungles of South America, just another scene. One of many that had Gloria Swann, Queen of Escapes bound and gagged and apparently helpless and at the mercy of her captors. It was to be Gloria's 'Swann song', as the cast and crew had laughingly called her latest motion picture epic. To Gloria however, it was to be her comeback.

Gloria's career had been faltering of late, and she was not so proud that she could not see it. The great roles she had played in the past were fewer, and more and more often her agent and manager had convinced her into taking lesser, smaller parts to help make ends meet and to pay her lavish bills. Gloria hated it, but as much as that was true, she loved living the high life that Hollywood had to offer, and in the end had conceded. She began taking the roles as the mother, the best friend, even taking the occasional bit as a nameless voice on a radio serial program or commercial. Anything to pay the creditors. It was when her agent presented her with the role of a grandmother, destined to die in a Roy Rogers western serial after only two lines, that she decided it was time to take action again and reclaim her life.

Gloria Swann had liquidated her assets and channeled her wealth into backing a new movie in which she would be the star. It would be a tribute to her career, and the films that had made her famous and a household name. An epic film that would have her fans clamoring for more. She had assembled the greatest technicians that Tinsel Town had to offer including an award winning director, a top-notch camera operator, and her favorite stunt coordinator whom she had known and worked with for years. She had commissioned a script from several of Hollywood's greatest writers, though in the end she had chosen to use a story by a young and relatively unknown named John Willie who seemed to have a natural affinity for bondage, if not escape. Gloria had rented and purchased all that would be necessary to create her opus, calling in old markers to reserve a studio sound stage for her private use and getting permission to actually travel to South America for real authenticity from a friend in American Customs. Within weeks it had all come together.

And it had been going so well. Certainly there was some tension. They were all jealous of her talent, of course, and her natural, if now mature beauty. Especially that upstaging little snot, Angela Morgan, her stand-in and stunt double. True, she was good at escaping from the perilous stunts that Karl Braun had thought up to expand on the initial script, and Angela's resemblance to Gloria was uncanny, or at least would have been twenty years prior in the star's youth. But Gloria was sure that the girl was out to take her job and status, to become the new Queen of Escapes. The girl had the others following her lead too. Braun was putty in her hands, of course, as the two had to work so closely together. All of the women, from the Script Girl to the Nurse to all of the extras seemed to like her, though Gloria could not understand why. More obvious, all of the men on the picture lusted to get under her skirts, and thus, thought she could do no wrong. Gloria Swann saw what was happening, under her very nose, and she hated the scheming little brat for the hornet's nest that she was stirring up. Angela Morgan would find however, that Gloria Swann was far from ready to be put out to pasture.

But now she was in the hands of "real" Amazons in far better shape than the extras that were only playing at being Amazons, and the pace that they set was swift indeed. They had veered from the marked path where the film scenes were to be shot, and Gloria had quickly lost her bearings as the three sped through the dense jungle foliage. Gloria Swann had bounced along like a jewel on a charm bracelet for what seemed like hours, helpless and at the mercy of the trio of exotic, mysterious warrior women.

Despite the aching in her shoulders and the strain placed on her wrists and ankles Gloria had soon found herself drifting in and out of unconsciousness. She was hurting, hot and exhausted from her ordeal and struggling, and the wild, jostling ride through the steaming jungle had eventually taken its toll. Gloria lost all sense of time, and it was only when she felt the cool blanket of shade drape over her that she had found the force of will to focus her senses once more. She had woken to a dim, flickering darkness. Long distorted shadows played over old gray stone slick and slimy with mildew. She seemed to be in a tunnel, illuminated by a small flaming torch carried by the woman that was apparently in charge of her captors; the Amazon dressed in the black animal skins and golden bangles.

Gloria tried to struggle again, but her ministrations simply made her ache all the more. The native women ignored her feeble struggles and muffled cries for help, continuing down the dark passage to God knows where.

Gloria Swann woke once more, shivering in the cold, her mind reeling. She felt parched, and her skin was dry and chafed beneath the leather that bound her wrists so tightly. Her perspiration had evaporated, leaving her chilled and nauseous. Her teeth were chattering, or trying to about the strip of leather that served as her gag. She was on the floor she realized, as her sight began to focus on her surroundings. The stout carry pole had been removed from beneath her bonds and she was lying on her side on the rough, cold stone of some vast, dank cavern.

Gloria began to twist and pull at the strand of leather lashed about her raw wrists once more as she cast her gaze about the dimly lit chamber. She saw one of the women that had been carrying her off in the distance a few yards away, moving about the walls of the vast cave lighting torches ensconced in the wall in metallic brackets. With each torch that sprang to life Gloria could make out more of her strange surroundings. She craned her neck, trying to observe as much as she could, still working at her bonds, trying to remember all that she had learned about Escapology over the years.

She could not see the roof of the cavern it was so high and lost in the darkness, though she did see a pin prick of sunlight far overhead. The

"...Gloria could make out more of her...surroundings."

beam of light that shot down into the cave struck the ground at what appeared dead center, reflecting off of some circular surface littered with sparkling metals and jewels. It appeared to be part of a stage or platform, raised slightly off of the floor, with a dais of some sort upon that, flanked by two tall and stout poles that seemed carved with ghastly faces and other images that she could not make out. There were things hanging from the walls as well, and littering the floor that she could see. Shields and weapons, bits of armor and wooden chests and crates, some of which that were open and heaping with trinkets of gold and jewels in all the colors of the rainbow. There was a vast fortune just lying about, and Gloria felt her pulse quicken as she thought of all that she could do with such wealth.

What truly caught her eye, however, was the massive statue that slowly faded into being with each new torch that was lit. It stood over twelve feet tall, a great massive thing that seemed carved of obsidian it was so black. It sparkled however, shining like dark ice in the flickering light, giving it a sense of movement and life in the firelight. It was shaped like a man, but as Gloria stared she saw that its head was that of a cat, like a gigantic panther, and its arms and legs ended in claws of ivory. Its eyes were inset jewels, rough chiseled slashes of green that seemed to burn in the darkness, returning her gaze. Gloria trembled, feeling as though those eyes were burning into her very soul.

Gloria had grunted in surprise into her gag as rough hands suddenly snaked under her arms and hauled her to her feet. She had not even noticed the Amazon woman, and could do nothing as the warrior hefted her over one shoulder and carried her onto the stage only to roughly deposit her onto the raised dais. Within seconds she was joined by her two companions, the one placing the torch in a sconce at the side of the alter, the other, the leader carrying a large woven burlap sack. The leader had grunted commands to the others, and Gloria was lifted again and quickly slammed against one of the tall totems where the two proceeded to lash her down.

While one of the pair crouched at her feet, tying yet another cord about Gloria's legs and the thick totem pole, the other took her long knife and quickly slashed the bit of leather that had been binding her wrists for so long. Instantly Gloria felt the blood rushing back into her hands, making her fingers tingle and burn with life. The star ignored the needle-like pain assaulting her hands and tried to surge forward, hoping to overcome her captors. The Amazon woman simply chuckled at Gloria's attempt however, placing a hand on Gloria's chest and roughly shoving her back against the stout wooden pole. Gloria's head bounced against the old, hardened wood, and her head started to spin as the warrior grabbed her wrists and wrenched her arms back behind the pole. Gloria moaned into her gag as she felt a knew length of leather being wrapped tightly about her wrists, effectively pinning her to the totem. Gloria struggled against the bonds that held her fast, feeling the cord snaking up her legs even as another was being wrapped about her midsection. A final bit of leather was bound about her throat, forcing her head back against the pole and holding it in place, restricting her breathing. When the two women finally stepped away Gloria Swann found herself immobile and more helpless than ever, bound to the totem pole like some sacrificial lamb and still gagged.

When Gloria finally stopped her struggles and admitted defeat, at least for the moment, she focused on the third of her trio of captors. The leader of the Amazons was doing something at the dais a few feet away. She had used a smoldering taper to alight several small tins of incense, and the air in the cavern was filling with a vaporous smoke that was slowly spiraling up and away through the hole in the roof. Still, the odorous vapors invaded Gloria's senses, and she soon found her mind reeling. It was not unlike the effects of opium, which she had experienced once during a trip to London when she was just starting out years ago. Her vision was starting to blur, and she felt her body starting to relax. In her drug-induced stupor, her captors appeared larger than life and leering, evilly hunkering about. Gloria tried shutting her eyes, but her head just started to spin faster and she was forced to try and focus on something lest she sick up.

The woman was mumbling something, chanting, and holding up something before the huge statue of the cat-man. Gloria tried to struggle as she saw the Amazon turn, the thing in her hands glowing as though radiating heat. It was golden, oval-shaped and carved into the image of a face; a cat's face. It was a mask, and as the warrior approached her, Gloria knew that it was meant for her. Gloria felt fingers intertwine in her hair at both ears, pulling her head back against the pole and holding her still. She struggled to no avail as the leader of the women raised the mask, and placed it over her face.

Gloria Swann screamed as the world flashed white. There was no pain, but her mind swam, suddenly awash by images, memories that she had never experienced. She saw flashes of herself, small and clumsy, running through the jungle. She saw her hands as she speared a wild pig; blood splattering her arms and warm on her face. Later, and an old woman was draping a golden necklace about her throat. She stared down at the glittering cat's head pendent, surrounded by golden claws. She saw dozens of women bowing down in this very cavern before the statue, the monument to *Nekara, El Gato Negra*, the black cat and God of the Cult of the Jaguar. How she knew this, Gloria could not say, but her mind screamed as the images pushed her own aside, taking over her thoughts.

Gloria slumped in her bonds, her heart hammering in her chest, her pulse racing a mile a minute. Through bleary eyes she tried to focus, her head slowly falling back into order, something that she could control. She felt the hands release her hair, and she swung her head about, shaking it to clear her jumbled thoughts. Her gaze fell on the leader once more, standing before her, hands on her hips in arrogant triumph. She seemed different somehow, smaller perhaps, and paler. Her raven black hair had faded to a dull, curly brown, shorter and framing a gilded face of gold. It took Gloria a moment to realize that the Amazon was wearing a mask that mirrored her own.

Gloria felt her clothes being cut and ripped away as the woman stared at her. The actress was not sure what exactly was happening, but she was starting to get a horrible idea. Her shirt was cut away, her corset and skirt sliced more carefully from her body eventually leaving the bound and gagged actress wearing only her imported French silk slip, brassiere and boots. Gloria saw the two Amazons that had tied her to the pole scurry off to one side where they set about repairing the torn and cut garments. The leader however stared at Gloria's semi-naked body for a moment longer. Behind the mask, Gloria could not tell what the woman was thinking, but her dark eyes seemed to burn with a hunger, glistening in the wavering torchlight. Finally, after a tense eternity, the leader of the Amazons reached up and gingerly pried the golden mask from her own face.

Gloria Swann stared, a growing horror swelling in her chest. Her body was shaking as the woman before her smiled wickedly, finally tossing the golden mask aside and starting to laugh. It was a cold and vile sound, made all the worse as Gloria slowly realized that the voice that she was hearing was her own. The body, the face; every feature of the mocking woman made her blood freeze. It was like looking into a dark mirror. It was like meeting her evil twin.

Gloria stared at the twisted, mocking face that was her own and screamed. The thin bit of leather stuffed into her mouth as a gag did little to muffle the sounds of her terror, and the echoes seemed a long time to die.

❀ ❀ ❀

Jonathan Harkins shielded his eyes against the harsh glare of the setting sun as he stared into the darkening jungle. Anger boiled within him, an irritating madness that had him biting on the bit of his cigar with such a force that he could feel his teeth grinding together. Gloria Swann had mucked him over once again, and he was really getting tired of it.

Harkins stalked along the trail through the jungle, his squinting eyes scanning the script in his hand as he watched peripherally about him. He had the crew searching, looking for any signs of where Gloria, Miss High and Mighty, Swann might have disappeared to. All around him, hidden in the undergrowth, he could hear the familiar voices as they called her name, over and over. Harkins knew how pointless it was, but he let it continue none the less, if only for show. The cast and crew of the movie were getting nervous, and maybe just a little scared. Too many queer things had been happening recently. Too many odd occurrences that could not be simply coincidence; like the mysterious arrows, or the animal that had trashed the camp and set that night the first week in the jungle.

Harkins knew however, that this was probably not connected. This was just Gloria Swann simply trying to remind him that she was indispensable. She was off somewhere having a temper tantrum over her lines, or a scene, or perhaps a jealous fit over her stand-in, the Morgan girl. Harkins had worked with Gloria enough to know the signs. She had done the same thing too many times to count. She was little better than a spoiled brat, a little rich girl that would hold her breath until she turned blue if she did not get her way.

Harkins was surprised that she had gone to the extent of actual physical violence though. Gloria was a great actress when it came to off camera histrionics. Usually, no matter the director or producer, if she yelled and fussed and stamped her feet loudly enough she would get her way. She had never actually resorted to hitting anyone. At least not hard enough to hurt them. But she had hit Jennifer Higgins, the Third Amazon. Hit her hard enough to knock her unconscious and draw blood.

Jonathan Harkins stopped in the small clearing where the cameras were being set up for the next shot and stared at the Higgins girl. She was still sitting on the mossy rock near where they had found her not long before. She had been out cold on the ground, a small puddle of blood matting her tousled brown hair. The cameraman Hunt had found her, along with the other two Amazon extras, but there had been no sign of Gloria. Kathy Parker had tended the girl's wounds, which apparently looked worse than they actually were. Higgins would have a right and proper goose egg on the back of the noggin for a day or two, but Carol Page was fairly certain that she could make it invisible on film.

Parker, the company nurse was still swabbing at the girl's scalp with cotton soaked in alcohol. The Amazons were hovering about nervously as well as the Morgan girl, all apparently concerned over the well being of their friend. Higgins was well liked, and had always seemed congenial to Harkins, though he had said nothing to her beyond the usual direction that he gave everyone else. He was far too busy to get involved with anyone, least of all a young wanna-be actress barely half his age. He did not imagine that she was lying when she said that she did not know what had happened. She had been hit on the head, after all. Harkins could not believe that Swann had staged the whole thing either, not that she was not capable of such a thing. No, somehow Gloria Swann, the Queen of Escapes had actually remembered the skills that had made her famous, had escaped from the ropes that had bound her and managed to cold cock the Higgins girl before disappearing into the jungle in order to give him an ulcer. She was probably watching them now, laughing her over-sized ass off.

Harkins grumbled as Shirley hustled past depositing a sheet of paper into his hands; a change to the script's next shot, sans Gloria. He scanned the paper, nodding his approval with a frown. It was not outlandish, but necessary. They were on a schedule, after all. They had enough shots of Gloria in bondage in the can. Close ups of Gloria gagged, bound with rope-thick and thin, leather, and writhing in various positions. Gloria was not necessary to the next scene, and his crew was good enough to work around her, or rather, the lack of her. Gloria had paid for the best crew available, and that was what she got. They would adjust the cameras and lighting, alter the set, and use Angela Morgan to the best of her abilities. Gloria Swann was a great actress, but she was not as indispensable as she thought.

Harkins stopped at the group surrounding the Higgins girl and smiled, just enough to show some concern.

"How are we?" he asked, trying to sound sincere. Higgins smiled back weakly, wincing as Parker dabbed at her scalp with a cotton swab.

"I'm all right, Mister Harkins." Harkins smirked, puffing on his cigar as Parker nodded in the background that it was true. Kathy Parker knew what she was doing, and Harkins trusted her professional opinion, more or less. As long as it did not interfere with getting his movie made.

"Well, get some rest Higgins. We don't need you in the next shot, but we will need you tomorrow, without a bandage wrapped about your head."

Higgins laughed, instantly regretting it as a wave of pain twisted her face and she grabbed at her temples. Parker would give the girl something for that, hopefully, and something to help her sleep. She would be ready tomorrow, he was sure. The girl; all the girls were troopers.

"All right people, we're losing the light! Let's get this next shot over with! And unless our glorious leading lady decides to suddenly grace us with her presence all eyes will be focused on our more than capable stand-in, Angela. Do try your best to make her look good people!"

Harkins smiled as the clearing suddenly came alive with activity. The crew forgot the search for Gloria Swann, now intent on doing their job, setting up for the next shot. He did so love being in charge.

Angela Morgan winced as the rope bit into her wrists. She thought that Karl Braun was tying her up a bit too severely, but he was the stunt coordinator, and she had trusted him with her life more times than she could remember. He had to know what he was doing, and what was best.

It was the last series of shots that she would have to endure running through the jungle. Of that she was glad. Angela felt that she had lost twenty pounds just in the last week, in the sweltering heat and humidity, not to mention from the exertion. She felt too that she would heal from the scars on her legs. Her skirt was long and thick, but her calves were scratched seemingly beyond repair, and she had developed a slight rash along her upper thigh. She still did not know how that had happened, but Kathy had given her a cream that had so far kept it at bay, if not under control.

"Ah!" she yelped as Karl knotted off the cord, securing her wrists behind her back again. Immediately Angela began to rotate her wrists and reach for the ropes, straining her fingers to pick at the knots. It was something she did unconsciously, practiced by rote over countless hours of being bound. It was something she loved, beyond the action and adventure of the acting. The bondage excited her, but the escape thrilled her, left her breathless.

"Engel…"

Angela gasped, looking up to see her friend and mentor staring at her with his cool gray eyes. His face was filled with concern as he watched her struggle against the ropes, but he made no move to help her or set her free.

"Are you all right?" he asked, wiping her hair from her eyes. "You seem a little out of breath."

"I'm fine. Just a little hot." In truth she was still a bit weak and feverish from her struggles in the river and the drug that had been on the dart that Kathy had pulled from her neck. Kathy had told her of her suspicions, that maybe the locals weren't so happy that the film company had invaded their jungle, and that had made her nervous. She knew though that the others were counting on her and she was determined to see her way through to the end. Especially now with Gloria missing.

Karl nodded with a smile. He knew more than he cared to admit Angela suspected, but he would never say so. He helped her to her feet, and together they walked towards her mark. She had gone over the trail already, twice in fact to make sure that she had memorized the markers along the way.

As far as stunts went, it was not very complicated. Angela was to run down the trail, hands bound behind her back, with the Amazons hot on her heels. She had just escaped from their temple, according to the script, and was running through the jungle in a desperate attempt to reach the encampment of her fellow explorers. It was rather shallow that bit, as far as stories went, but it was right up the alley of what Gloria Swann's fans expected. Scene after scene of harried action, adventure and bondage. Angela did not expect to win any awards, either for herself or Gloria, but she would do her best.

Karl pointed out where the cameras were situated as they walked to her starting point. One would follow her from behind, giving the audience a good view of her bound wrists as though from the Amazon's point of view. Another would catch her about midway through her run as she charged through the brush. She would need to remember exactly where that camera would be so as not to look surprised when she saw it, nor look directly into the lens and thus spoil the illusion that she was Gloria. The third and final camera was set up on a wooden platform actually nestled up in the branches of a tree. It would be trained on her most of the way, and it was that one that she had to keep in mind. She must not deviate from the path and get out of the frame.

Besides the run itself, there would be several jumps along the way. Nothing spectacular, but more than Gloria would be expected to do. Angela had to leap over several fallen logs, across a gap from stone to stone, and over a short embankment. A simple stunt, and easy money in her purse.

"Children...Children!" Angela turned to see Harkins barking into his megaphone, his entourage ready to bolt as they all hovered about him. Alice and Martha stood with two of the other Amazon extras that Angela did not know as well. They stood at their marks, ready to run along behind, and eventually pass the camera that Jimmy Barton would be chasing her with. Shirley Compton smiled, her perfect teeth sparkling as she gave Angela a little wave of encouragement, script in hand. She felt Karl's hand on her shoulder as the director ordered everyone to their places.

"Do good, Engel." Angela smiled as her boss walked away, his feet slipping a bit in the soft earth. It was hot out again, despite the fact that the sun was about to drop below the horizon. They had to get this shot in one take, because it would be too dark to try again after the first. The air would be thick with mosquitoes by then as well, and god knew what other creatures roaming the jungle. Of everything that she hated on this jungle adventure, she thought that she hated the hungry, relentless insects most of all.

"Ready, people! Let's get this in one, shall we?" Jonathan settled into his canvas chair and gave the script a final glance as Shirley held up a dimly lit lantern for him to see by. Jimmy Barton secured the panels on his camera and spun his Brooklyn Dodgers cap backwards as he lined Angela up in his viewfinder, ready to run. Jackson Walters would be running alongside Jimmy, running interference as it were. The path had been cleared of low branches and jutting roots and rocks, but still, with Jimmy looking through the camera he would be almost blind. Jackson would be his eyes, trying to direct Jimmy along the course.

"Mark!"

Angela stood ready as Shirley slapped the marker for the scene, announcing the time, shot and take. Angela saw lanterns flare off scene, and a moment later a crank generator hummed with energy. Light splashed along the trail setting the clearing aglow like noon.

"Read lights!" Jonathan shouted, holding a small lens up to his eye and squinting through. "Cameras ready! Roll one!" Angela saw Jimmy start cranking on his camera to get it going. It would take a few seconds for the gears and mechanisms to lock into place, and another few moments for Jimmy to focus on her again. "Roll two!" Jonathan bellowed into his megaphone, and she knew that somewhere down the trail Joseph Hunt was grinding away at his own camera now, up in the trees. The third and final camera would only start recording when John Thomas, the Assistant Director saw Angela clearly running down the trail.

"Quiet people...Ready..." Angela braced.

"Action!"

Angela Morgan ran down the trail for all she was worth. Harkins had told her that Jimmy Barton would not be able to keep up, but that was fine. She should try to outdistance him, to give the illusion that she was escaping her pursuers. She could hear Jimmy and Jackson charging after her, but already lagging behind. She could hear Alice and Martha as well as the other two women, keeping pace behind the young cameraman, ready to rush past him.

Angela saw her first marker and leapt, legs churning through the air a short distance before landing hard on another stone a few feet away. She scrambled to get her feet beneath her, not an easy task with her hands bound behind her back, but she managed not to fall. She kept running.

Birds cried out in the trees over head and she heard monkeys chattering madly at her passing. The jungle was just coming awake, it seemed, and soon the great cats would be on the prowl; the panther and the jaguar. She wanted this to be over before the predators were out in force, if they were not already. She slid down a slight incline and ran beneath the camera set in the trees. Soon she would hear Alice or Martha cry out and she would have to pick up her pace again.

Angela jogged left, passing the second marker and dashed off into the trees. She did not recall the turn being so sharp, but then she had not been going as fast when she walked the course with Karl before. She was sweating already too, and she could hear the mosquitoes buzzing about her ears hungrily, drawn by her body heat. She was well past the halfway point, but she still had the final long leap to go, and she needed to conserve her energy for that, so she held back despite her urge to outrun the insects.

Oddly, the jungle seemed to get thicker as she went, denser than she remembered. The trail seemed harder to follow with every step, and she was sure that she should have reached her next marker by now. She should have seen Thomas and the third camera crew as well. Angela slowed, suddenly worried that she had strayed from the path, listening for direction. She heard someone shouting her name far behind her.

Angela screamed as the ground suddenly broke and fell away beneath her. There was a deafening crack and crash of wood, and she was falling amidst a hail of tree limbs and matted grass, leaves fluttering. She heard something growl, drowning out her own startled scream as she hit the ground, landing hard on her hip. Pain shot through her body as she collapsed in a heap, debris falling down about her. Her vision whirled, spinning gray and exploding in bursts of throbbing darkness.

Angela moaned as she tried to sit up. Her left leg was throbbing, but it did not feel broken. Still, she was in pain and dizzy with sudden nausea.

She wondered what had happened.

She looked up and around, trying to determine where she was. She did not remember a hole being along the route, so she surmised that she must have taken a wrong turn, missed a marker. How, she did not know. Not that the 'how' mattered. It had happened, and she was sitting in a hole, a pit almost ten feet deep.

Angela heard movement, heavy breathing. Something growled a hungry, guttural thing. Angela stared into the dark corners of the pit, her eyes growing wide as she saw the shadows swirl and start to move. Something black slithered through the darkness, sleek, shining muscles glistening in the slight strands of light filtering down from above. Glowing slits of greenish amber flickered, considering her as they shifted from side to side. She saw a flash of white as something growled again.

Angela Morgan gasped as the great black panther padded into the circle of light at the center of the pit. Her heart slammed in her chest, threatening to explode. She saw the beast lick its muzzle as it stared at her, hunger burning in its eyes.

Angela screamed as it pounced.

EPISODE FIVE:
THE FLIGHT TO DANGER!

*A*ngela Morgan rolled to the side, falling to the cold, packed earth as the great beast pounced. Fear and instinct prodded her to kick out, an instinct for survival more than any skill. Pain ran up her legs as her heels rammed into the big cat's chest and throat. It yowled in a pain of its own as it spun in midair and slammed against the wall of the pit before bouncing away again, scrambling back into the shadows of the far side of the wide hole.

The panther snarled, licking its muzzle as it shook its head. Eyeing her suspiciously, the beast began to pace, back and forth, left and right. She had stunned it, more than hurt it Angela suspected, and it would be upon her again within seconds as soon as it judged her threat potential.

Angela struggled to rise, pressing against the wall of the pit as she inched her way back to her feet. Her leg was throbbing worse now than before, and sweat poured from her, matting her hair and stinging her eyes. She was terrified, watching as the great cat padded the wide pit, prowling. Her wrists twisted and turned in the confines of her bonds. Her fingers danced over the knots in the ropes, tugging and pulling at any stray thread that might set her free. She had to get out, get away before the panther sprang to attack again.

"Angela!"

She heard the voice calling her name, and cautiously Angela shifted her gaze to the lip of the pit above. She tried to call out, but her voice caught in her throat. Even that slight noise caused the huge black panther to snarl and hunker. She slumped against the wall again with a gasp as it crouched in the darkness, ready to strike.

Something came crashing down into the pit, causing Angela and the panther both to scream in surprise. Angela staggered away, hugging the wall as she stared at the huge stone that had been thrown from above and was suddenly imbedded in the dirt at her feet. She chanced a glance up again, as the panther began its frantic pace once more, now seeming more frenzied and trapped. Angela gasped to see Harkins standing at the edge of the pit, watching. Jimmy Barton was there as well, and Harkins was whispering something in his ear, his hand on the boy's shoulder. Jimmy was cranking furiously at his camera, and Angela suddenly realized that they were filming what might well be the last moments of her life. She screamed for help.

A loop of rope dropped down into the pit, encircling Angela about the shoulders as she staggered, keeping away from the cat. Her eyes were wide with fright, and she wondered what new terror this was going to be when the lasso tightened about her, pressing into her breasts and squeezing the breath out of her lungs. She did not have time to think as she was suddenly hoisted off of her feet and into the air. She saw the cat leap at her as hands snaked under her armpits and powerful arms quickly hefted her up and out of the pit. She felt the panther's claws as the beast swatted at her feet, and she swiftly swung her legs out of the hole and out of reach.

Angela slammed onto the ground, the breath driven from her even as she tried to scream once more and scramble away. Shadowy forms hovered above her in the waning light, reaching for her as hands pawed at her body. She felt the lasso being lifted over her head, and someone was undoing the knots that held her wrists as a familiar voice clucked at her with concern.

"Engel! Are you all right!"

She stared blankly, numbness draping over her like a blanket as she realized just how close to death she had been. Someone was pulling at her, trying to drag her away from the pit as voices shouted about her, raised in anxiety. As through a fog she saw Karl settling her back against a tree. He wrapped a blanket about her shoulders, hugging her to keep her warm. She was going into shock.

Angela saw Harkins directing Jimmy back and away from the edge of the pit as two burly men with guns strode forward. It was De Grassi and Trent, two of the company stagehands that had come along on the shoot. She watched as the men leveled rifles at the beast, still trapped in the pit, but she heard Harkins shouting at them, ordering them to wait. Jimmy was still filming.

The panther sprang from the pit, and Angela screamed along with almost everyone else. Harkins scrambled back and away as De Grassi fell under the cat's swift, sudden attack. His gun flew from his hands as he collapsed under the panther's weight, sharp claws ripping at his flesh. Trent screamed, backing up and waving his own rifle about as he tried to get a bead on the creature that would not also hit his friend. Angela heard Jennifer and Kathy screeching in the background; all the women were hysterical. De Grassi's shrill cries rose above all the others however, as the cat clawed and bit at the struggling stagehand.

Angela heard the report of a gun just as Karl stepped between her and the grisly scene. There was a shrill cry of agony, then more screams of terror and Angela saw a fleet, dark shadow disappear, lunging into the jungle brush. There was much confusion then, screaming and shouting, and everything seemed to be spiraling into a flurry of motion. Angela felt her head grow light, and then her vision grayed to black.

"I say we get out."

Jonathan Harkins bit down on his cigar, trying his best not to grind his teeth in aggravation. He was standing with his back to the group, that select few that he had gathered that he actually listened to concerning the filming of the movie. He stared out through the mosquito netting covering the flap of the Mess Tent where they were meeting. Beyond, the jungle was dark and mysterious as usual, but alive with noise and life just hidden out of sight. He could hear the low rumble of the river and falls not so far away, and if he strained, occasionally he could hear the tortured mewling of the panther, off somewhere in the darkness licking its wounds.

"Mein Gott, Jonathan! Someone is trying to kill us!"

Harkins turned, leveling a steely gaze at the stunt master. Karl Braun was sitting on one of the small canvas stools scattered about the tent, returning the director's stare without flinching. He was wringing wet with sweat staining his shirt and running down his face. Just looking at the older man made Harkins aware of the perspiration running down his own back. The humidity was high again, and the air was thick and moist, just a heartbeat away from rain that would never seem to come. The older man took a drag off of his cigarette, grimacing at the taste as blue smoke billowed about him.

"Karl. I think that if someone…some indigenous native was trying to kill us…well…I hazard to guess that we'd all be dead by now. 'Gott' knows they've had every opportunity to do so." Harkins smirked, but Karl Braun was apparently not amused by his mocking little joke. "That pit was probably left over from some tribe that's long since moved on. That cat probably just stumbled into it some time ago, and poor Angela stumbled in after. Coincidence is all."

"It was covered up, Jonathan. Angela said that she didn't see it at all." Braun took another drag from his cigarette, then dropped it into the dirt and crushed it out under the toe of his cowboy boot. "And what about the markers? I walked that trail myself, marking it off for Angela's run. The markers were changed; moved."

"Karl…" Harkins shook his head, smiling as warmly as he could. "Karl. I think you must be mistaken. You *are* getting old, my friend, and even I admit that after a few days in this hellish jungle, it all starts looking alike. You must have placed the markers wrong, or maybe Angela simply got confused. I like her too, but she's not perfect."

Harkins saw Braun's skin redden as anger swelled within him. The older man started to rise, and the director considered for a moment that he might have said too much, but before he could apologize, John Thomas was on his feet between the two men. The assistant director placed a hand on the stunt coordinator's shoulder, holding him down and in place, but turned his attention on Harkins.

"It's your final decision of course, Jonathan, but you have to consider all of this. The markers, the pitfall, our food stores spoiling a few days ago and the animals wrecking the camp. There were those arrows shot at Gloria and Angela too, that no one could account for. Now we have a wounded animal prowling about the vicinity, and Bill De Grassi hurt. Thank God he wasn't injured beyond Kathy's abilities to mend or even killed. What about that?"

Harkins turned to Kathy Parker, the crew nurse and looked at her

"Mein Gott, Jonathan, someone is trying to kill us!"

expectantly. Kathy shrugged.

"Bill will live. He won't be carrying anything for awhile, but I cleaned the wounds and stitched them up. They looked worse than they really were."

"See?" Harkins waved his arms about, trying to prove his point. "We're fine. I have men out looking for that cat, and I'm sure that it'll be dead before we're done in here even."

"And what about Gloria?" Joseph Hunt stood up and drew the attention of all in the tent. He had remained silent at first, a trait he was used to as senior cameraman, but apparently he could no longer remain silent. "Gloria's still out there somewhere, maybe hurt or lost. What are we gonna do about her?"

Harkins smirked, biting down on his cigar again. "Gloria is fine. I've known her far longer than some of our crew has been alive, and I know when our star is off having a tantrum." Jonathan Harkins tried to sound sure of himself, but in reality, he was starting to have some doubts about the star of the picture himself. Harkins had expected her back long before now, her tirade at an end, but she had not materialized. Now he was starting to wonder. "Gloria will be back, rest assured, unscathed and bitchy as ever."

Harkins scanned the crowd, smiling his best smile. He still saw doubt, but the crew was teetering in his direction, even though he had really said nothing to explain away the strange occurrences. All except Braun, and he would vote with the majority in the end. They were so close to wrapping up that Harkins could almost taste it. He would be damned if they folded up camp now.

"Listen, we only have a handful of shots left. The plane should be here tomorrow, and we can get close-ups until it's ready, then shoot the scenes on the plateau if we have to. We're going to finish up here people, if I have to put on a wig and a dress and crank the bloody camera myself! If Gloria 'Miss High and Mighty' Swann deigns to rejoin us, all the better. But I will not lose this film! Is that…"

Gunshots split the night, setting the jungle to a frenzied life with noise. Monkeys screamed in a panic, and birds swarmed into the humid air, a dark swirling cloud passing before the waxing moon. All eyes turned towards the camp beyond the tent. Harkins could see others emerging from other tents to see what was happening, and he quickly pushed the thin netting aside and stepped outside as well.

Mosquitoes set upon him instantly, despite the foul-smelling oils that he and the rest smeared on their exposed skin every few hours. Harkins ignored the biting insects and dashed across the compound, stopping alongside the Morgan girl and the three Amazon extras that had come out of their tent. Her eyes were still wide from her earlier encounter with the panther, but Harkins thought that she seemed a little better. Still, he noted the tremble in her voice when she spoke.

"Wh...was that a gun?"

Jennifer Higgins placed a hand on Angela's shoulder and gave her a gentle squeeze. Her friend was still rattled, and rightly so. Jennifer thought that she might well be in a coma after going head on with a tiger. She admired Angela though, that she was up and ready to go already, if only a little worried. Jennifer imagined that was why she was a stunt woman. She had nerves of steel.

"Maybe it was thunder," Jennifer offered, though she really did not believe it. She had heard enough gunfire on enough movie serial sets of Westerns to know the difference between a gunshot and a peal of thunder. She just hoped that the gunfire did not signal still more trouble.

"No!" Alice Simmons, one of the Amazon extras, said with some excitement as she pointed towards the trail leading into the jungle. "Look!"

Everyone stared to where she was pointing, and in a moment saw four shadows moving through the underbrush. Trent was first, walking ahead of the group looking filthy with dirt and slick with sweat. He was carrying three rifles, and soon enough it was apparent why. Following behind the stagehand was Jimmy Barton and Phil Turner the inside prop-man, the two men supporting the weight of the limp panther carcass between them. Even in the dim light outside of the compound Jennifer could see that the animal's sleek fur was lathered and slick with blood.

What caught her eye however was the fourth figure staggering along behind the three grinning men. They were apparently oblivious, beaming with pride over their kill, and only when the mystery person stumbled and fell with a crash behind them did they spin about in surprise, Barton and Turner actually dropping the big cat. Trent let two of the rifles he was carrying fall to the ground as he brought the third to bear before he realized what was going on. Like a mob, the crew surged forward, Jennifer swept along in its motion. Jennifer heard herself shouting.

"My god! It's Gloria!"

Angela Morgan stopped and took a swig of tepid water from her canteen. It was warm and brackish, but still quenched her thirst, and she was thankful that Kathy Parker had insisted that everyone carry their own water. She resealed the cap and stared up at the plateau, shielding her eyes from the glare of the sun. It was barely eight in the morning, but the sun was already blazing brightly, forcing her to squint. The air was not so thick with humidity however, and for that she was glad. It was still hot, and she was still sweating, but it was better than it had been the day before.

She turned her gaze to the top of the plateau that loomed ahead, still over a mile away. It was impressive, though barely over a hundred feet high, still it rose almost like an anvil over the jungle. It was wide as well; wide enough to land an aeroplane on, apparently, as the entire camp, give or take a few members, were going to meet the biplane scheduled for use in the movie up on top.

A chill ran up and down Angela's spine as she recalled the upcoming stunt involving the biplane and the plateau, and her as well. From there on the jungle trail the plateau looked imposing. From above, dangling from a rope beneath the aeroplane, she could only imagine that it looked threatening at the very least.

"Penny for 'em."

Angela Smiled as Jennifer Higgins strolled up beside her. Like Angela, and almost everyone else, she was carrying a load of necessary movie equipment along the trail that the crew had to hike. It was over five miles from the falls to the plateau, most of it uphill, and in the sweltering heat of the jungle, it was almost like murder. Jennifer was dressed like most of the women, wearing denim pants, boots and a thick blouse. There had been a bit of an argument with Kathy Parker as most of the women had wanted to cut down the leggings of the slacks, but the nurse had been adamant that they should not expose their skin to the sun, or the insects, not to mention the strange and exotic plants that they would be tromping through along the trail. In the end Kathy had won out, and everyone was wrapped up against the sun, flora and fauna.

"Just thinking about the stunt, Jenny. In a few hours I'll be dangling from a rope up there somewhere."

"You're not scared?"

"Petrified! But that's why I make the big bucks." Angela elbowed her friend in the ribs and together they started off again, laughing. There were a couple dozen people in the line marching to the plateau, and only a few remained behind at the base camp where they had done most of the filming. Kathy was one of those, remaining behind to watch over Bill De Grassi who was still recovering from being mauled by the panther. Trent had stayed behind as well, with a few of the hands as well as two of the editors to help protect the camp, and Kathy and Bill, until the final shots were in the can. Angela suspected that Trent also wanted time to skin the cat that he had shot, saving them all.

Angela glanced up the trail as they hiked, the plateau looming slowly closer with every step. She saw Harkins at the head of the group, surrounded by his entourage; Shirley Compton the script girl, John Thomas the assistant director, and Joseph Hunt, the senior cameraman. Karl was up there as well, along with Carol Page, the make-up girl, going over something in the script. Gloria was up there too, though oddly she was marching along behind the rest. Stranger still, she was actually helping carry some of the equipment that had to be lugged from the base camp to the top of the plateau. Angela had thought that 'help' was one of those words stricken from Gloria's vocabulary.

When Gloria had come stumbling into the camp the night before, everyone had suspected the worst. Kathy had been on her in an instant however, and after a quick inspection had declared that Gloria was suffering from exposure to the sun and dehydration. The movie star had some scrapes and cuts, but Kathy Parker had said that they were 'superficial', and not life threatening. Everyone was elated of course, especially after what had happened to Bill De Grassi earlier in the day, but Gloria herself was almost comatose, and Kathy had prescribed that rest was her best bet at that point.

Gloria had slept the night away, while the stagehands started to load up the things needed to transport; lighting, cameras and film, special props and a couple tents. Come morning however, Gloria seemed alert and ready to move out with the rest of the crew. She was oddly silent, but that was a blessing really, as she was not complaining as usual. She had offered up some lame excuse of escaping her bonds and then getting lost for the time that she was missing, and everyone seemed to take her at her word, especially after what Harkins had said before. Most of the crew suspected that the entire ordeal was just one of Gloria's ploys to get attention, and Angela had to agree. Gloria had woken refreshed, taking up a load to carry and marching along the trail with the rest.

Angela stared daggers at Harkins, however. She could still see him standing on the edge of the pit, prompting Jimmy to continue filming while the great cat paced closer. Angela had been terrified, far worse than in any stunt she had ever done. Harkins had been ready to film her being mauled to death, and did not seem to even care. The film had to go on, apparently. He had not even apologized.

Angela's anger was pushed aside as a rattling, buzzing noise filled the sky. Almost as one the entire crew looked up and around, and one by one they began pointing towards the west above the treeline.

Like a great bird, the biplane swooped up above the trees, arching across the sky with an arrogant ease. It trailed smoke, and sputtered a bit as it banked, coming in from the sun, but still it looked magnificent, and was a firm reminder to all of civilization here in the wilds of the vast, isolated Brazilian jungle.

Angela shielded her eyes as she watched the biplane swerve, rocking its wings for the crowd below. She could just make out the concentric circles on the midsection, and numbers stenciled onto the tail marking it as a British war machine. Angela knew however that it was owned by the studio, bought as surplus after the First World War and had been used in many films since. She had even met the pilot once, on the set of another picture. He was a happy, older man formerly of Britain's Royal Air Force named Sebastian Pitt. He was retired now, but apparently he had been a hero in World War One, owning several kills; enemy fighters shot down in dogfights. Now he flew free lance for the studios and did the occasional Air Circus when he had the time. Pitt had given her the grand tour of the plane, offering to take her up sometime though they had yet to get together on that, so she knew that the plane was a De Havilland DH 82, with a wingspan of almost thirty feet and a range of over two hundred and seventy-five miles. "A grand machine!" Pitt had proclaimed, and Angela was sure that he was right, though she had thought it skinny and looking a bit frail for her tastes.

She knew that Pitt was flying the plane from the rear seat, so the passenger she saw in the front seat had to be Adam Kaine. Adam was technically the male lead of the picture, though in truth the movie was all about Gloria. As such, Adam had not really been needed through most of the filming, as he only had a few scenes at the beginning and then again at the end, in the movie's exciting climax. Still, Harkins had wanted him here in South America for some authentic shots in and around the plane.

Adam Kaine waved at the marching crowd as the plane dove then swooped up again right overhead, just missing the tops of the trees. Adam was handsome enough, Angela supposed, with his bronze skin, wavy dark hair and steely gray eyes, but he was just as arrogant as Gloria Swann, if not more so. He always had a starlet on his arm in public, but the rumor mill in Hollywood more than once suggested that he preferred men, and all too often 'young' men. It had never been proven, of course, but it was enough to make Angela hate him. Unfortunately, most other women found him appealing, and Angela was forced to shake her head and march on as her friends cheered and waved at his passing.

Starting up the trail that wound along the sheer side of the plateau, and a few yards into the inclined hike, Angela glanced up to see Gloria still staring as the aeroplane made its final run for landing. A look of awe was plastered on Gloria's face, making her look simple and childlike. She followed the biplane in flight with her eyes until it disappeared over the summit of the plateau, then rushed ahead of the crew with an energy that made Angela think she might run all the way to the top. Despite her harrowing experience, and the injuries that she had sustained, Angela thought that Gloria seemed overly energetic. She was barely sweating in the heat, and not breathing hard at all. She had a few scars about her legs, but her skin seemed darkly tanned, unlike everyone else who was peeling already from recurring burns. If anything, she seemed in better shape than before she had disappeared two days before.

"Let's go, Morgan. It's getting hot out here."

Angela felt Martha Johnson's gentle push and realized that she had been lost in thought. She smiled at the Second Amazon, then shuffled her feet to get back into the rhythm of the walk, shouldering her pack and bags. Up ahead, Jennifer was waiting beside a large rock just a few feet away, and Gloria was almost out of sight around a bend in the trail. Angela glanced up, shielding her eyes from the sun and sighed. There was still a long way to go.

Angela Morgan stood at the cliff's edge, staring out and down at the vast canopy of the jungle below. Far in the distance she could see where the river snaked its way through the trees, but the rest was like a huge, lumpy sheet of green stretching away to the pale, purple mountains to the west. The plateau had not looked quite so high from down below and even winding her way up the trail along its side it had not seemed too imposing. Standing atop the great, flat butte however, Angela was starting to wonder. It was not the height so much that bothered her, but falling from it. Not that the fall itself would kill her, but rather the abrupt stop at the end.

She turned away from the ledge and paced back towards her mark for the stunt, barely one hundred feet away. It was a simple enough stunt, in theory, but in actuality it was possibly the most dangerous that she had ever attempted. There was so much that could go wrong. According to

the script, she was to have run up the trail to the top of the plateau where
the hero would pick her up and take her away to safety. The Amazons
would be upon her, of course, and she would still be loosely bound as
she signaled the aeroplane circling overhead. Adam, actually Sebastian,
would then swoop down as the Amazons ran to catch her, firing their
arrows and throwing spears. He would come in low, and Angela would
have to grab onto the axle of the wheels and be carried off into the sky.
Sebastian would then lower a ladder and she would climb into the waiting
arms of her lover. Of course the final scene would be a close up of Gloria
and Adam lip-locked as the screen faded to black, the plane flying off into
the sunset. Roll credits.

Angela heard the biplane sputter to life and looked up as she reached her
mark. Karl was at the plane, of course, checking the axle and adding strips
of leather to give her a grip when she had to latch onto the plane. Sebastian
was in the pilot's seat, going over his own check list, preparing the plane
for the flight as he waved away Jimmy who had cranked the propeller to
life. Angela had every confidence in Sebastian, and trusted that he would
fly the biplane at the proper level for her to grab hold without cutting her
to ribbons in the propeller. He was a barn stormer and a crop duster, a
decorated World War One veteran. He would not let her down.

Angela was surprised to see Gloria standing beside the plane again.
Earlier she had run up the last bit of the trail to be on top of the plateau when
the biplane had landed. When the rest of the cast and crew had reached
the summit, Gloria was there at the plane, almost dancing about like a
child in awestruck wonder, as though she had never seen an aeroplane
before. She had bombarded Sebastian with questions, to the point where
the pilot had had to go into the latrine to get away from the movie star.
While the rest of the crew had set up a make-shift camp atop the plateau,
she had hovered about the plane like a vulture, actually getting into the
seats and playing with the controls, under Sebastian's guidance. She had
even ignored Adam Kaine, in favor of the pilot. It was all very odd, Angela
thought.

The biplane sputtered and coughed black smoke again, then started
rolling forward as everyone backed away to give it room. Karl jogged
towards her, occasionally glancing back as the De Havilland rolled towards
the edge of the plateau, picking up speed. Harkins had one camera trained
on the aeroplane throughout the takeoff and even through its practice
runs. Sebastian would fly by twice at least, judging the distance and the
wind, making sure that he had the approach down right, then if he was

satisfied, he would give a thumb's up sign that Angela would return if she too was ready.

Everyone watched as the biplane rolled on, faster and faster. There was a tense moment as the plane reached the edge of the plateau and seemingly started to fall, disappearing below the ledge for a moment. Angela heard someone scream but a second later the aeroplane swooped up, up and away, arching towards the west, and the slowly setting sun. Sebastian rocked the great machine, arrogantly letting everyone know that all was fine.

"Show off…" Karl mumbled as he stepped up beside Angela, watching as Sebastian put the biplane into a long, graceful banking curve. Satisfied that the biplane was not going to crash, he turned his attention to Angela and began adjusting the ropes loosely tied about her wrists. He smiled, gazing into her eyes, looking for weakness.

"You are sure about this, Engel? Just say the word and I will tell Harkins that the stunt is too dangerous."

Angela tried to speak, swallowed a lump in her throat. "I'll be fine, Karl. I trust Sebastian. I trust you. What could go wrong?" Angela smiled as Karl tightened the knots on the ropes loosely dangling from her wrists. In the picture, she was almost free, the once tight bonds now trailing about a foot between her wrists. Karl had bound her with her trick rope, the hollowed out, break away bit so that she would have full movement when she was trying to climb aboard the biplane.

They both looked up as the biplane flew by just overhead. Karl ducked down, but Angela stood her ground, trembling as the wheels whipped by within reach. The backdraft of the plane almost bowled her over and she was forced to stagger a few steps to regain her footing. She stared after the plane, watching as it banked up and around, circling in a wide arc to make another pass.

"This is ridiculous! I am going to tell Harkins to call this off." Karl Braun started to turn away, to head back to where Harkins was positioning the Amazons for the shot. Angela grabbed his arm.

"No, Karl! I want to do this. Unless you think I can't."

Karl looked glumly at his apprentice, obviously struggling with his own inner demons. "You can. I know you can. It's just…"

"Then leave it be, Karl. I'll be fine."

Karl looked at her for a long moment, and Angela tried her best to smile, to hide the fear that was making her legs ice and had her heart hammering in her chest. Finally he hugged her, kissing her on the cheek.

"Be safe, my Engel."

"Always…"

Angela watched as Karl reluctantly turned and walked away. Angela felt totally alone then. Alone with her fear. She saw Jennifer and the rest of the Amazons flexing their bows and taking their marks; ready to start running when the cameras were called to action. Gloria was watching the plane as it circled, readying for its next approach. She and Adam were sitting near Harkins in their own canvas-backed chairs, watching as the crew scurried about at the director's orders. They seemed totally calm, like the eye in a storm, and why not? Neither had a thing to do until Harkins was ready for the final scene. Angela saw John Thomas as well, far off across the plateau with Joseph Hunt, manning camera two. It was their job to track Angela as she ran towards the cliff's edge, keeping her in frame as she dangled underneath the plane.

Angela was forced to duck down as the biplane roared past again, a little lower than before. Her long, dirty skirt swirled in its wake, her hair blowing madly, but she was glad for the wind. The vast, empty top of the plateau was arid and the rays of the sun seemed to bounce off its surface, doubling in intensity. Angela was sweating bullets and her already filthy clothes were wringing wet and smelling very badly. Carol Page had patted her down with dust and dirt to make her look authentic, and had been adamant that she not rewash her hair after she had rinsed out her shock of white the night before last again. Angela felt that her skin was crawling, and she just knew that she was ridden with lice and fleas, not to mention covered with mosquito bites.

She tried to focus on the task at hand, however, watching as Sebastian arched the plane around in the other direction, judging the speed of the wind and currents in the air. She tried not to think of the propeller slicing into her if he came in too low, or her missing the axle or worse, catching it wrong. If she did not get a good grip, she might fall to her death off of the plateau, or be dragged behind the speeding plane. She saw Sebastian waving at her, giving her the 'thumb's up' signal. He was ready. Without thinking, Angela returned the sign before she could chicken out.

She focused intently on the plane then, blocking out distraction and watching as it banked up and around, making for its final run. Hunt's camera would be running now, trained on her, but Harkins only wanted the sequence of her running, so it did not matter what she did until she started her stunt. Angela took deep breaths as she waited, low in her diaphragm. The sun was pounding down on her, and her heart was thumping so loudly that it almost drowned out the roar of the plane. She gave a final glance to the crew, panning the crowd. Karl was closest, ready to run to her aid should she need it. Jennifer, Martha, Alice and the rest of the Amazons were braced to run, their cue when the biplane passed over them. Harkins was ready, his arm up and braced to cue her, but Karl had said to ignore the director this time. She would know best when it was time to start.

The plane pulled out of its curve, waggling a bit, then straitening out until it seemed to bear directly at her. It began its descent, and Angela tried to swallow, her mouth dry but a lump in her throat. She started to count, waiting until she could see Sebastian's face through the blur of the propeller, then she turned. She started to run.

Her breathing was raspy and labored. Her legs seemed heavy, as though she were running through molasses. All she could hear was the rattle of the plane getting closer and closer, and the echo of her heartbeat pounding in her ears. She glanced back, praying that she did not trip and fall. Karl had cleared her path earlier that morning, sweeping and picking away any danger, but still...

The biplane was leveled out and closer than she might have hoped. Angela felt her heart rise up in her chest, trying to force its way out her throat but clogging there, making it even harder to breathe. She heard someone shouting, off to the side and out of sight. An arrow drove into the ground several feet in front of her, then another spiraled away and out of sight over the cliff's edge. She had forgotten that the eight Amazons would be shooting at her. She willed herself to go on, faster, and chanced another glance over her shoulder.

Almost...

Angela raised her arms before her, ready to loop her right arm about the axle as Karl had told her. It would not be pretty, but editing would make her, Gloria, rather, look spectacular in the end. All she had to do was snap the trick rope apart and grab on, holding for dear life. That was all.

Almost...

Angela ran, glancing back, arms akimbo as she tugged at the loosely bound ropes encircling her wrists. She still wore the leather gloves that Karl had given her to hide her wounds from a few days past that had still not quite healed. Her muscles ached from fighting the river and the constant running. She had vivid memories of falling into the pit, the panther attacking her. She was battered and bruised, tired and hot but she pushed it all aside, every ache and pain, running. Adrenaline spurred her forward. That and terror.

The propeller whipped her hair about and Angela stretched, groping blindly while she ducked, almost running sideways. Angela screamed as the plane's axle slammed into her funnybone. Pain shot through her body as tears welled in her eyes. She bit down on her cheek, gritting her teeth as she tried to ignore the pain. Angela looped her arm about the axle, gripping her wrist with her free hand to lock it in place. She staggered along, trying desperately to pace the much faster plane, racing it. She stumbled and fell, hanging on as a new pain ran through her arm. The axle was hot, and the leather grip that Karl had attached hurt and pulled at her skin. She felt her feet fall away beneath her, felt the gravel and dirt of the plateau eating through the soft leather of her boots as she was dragged along. She was in agony…crying… wanting to let go…

And suddenly she was flying.

Angela felt the ground vanish beneath her and suddenly she was kicking her feet in open air. She felt the wind whipping about her, jostling her about as she clung to the bottom of the plane for dear life. She could smell burning oil, feel the heat of the engine that roared and rattled in her ears. She opened her eyes, not even realizing that she had clenched them shut, fearful of what she might see, but afraid that she might miss the wildest ride of her life.

The world stretched out below her, rolling away to the horizon in soft waves, like a verdant ocean. The sun sparkled brightly, high in the sky once more, its fierce heat just a bitter memory. The wind lashed at her, stinging the bare skin of her arms and legs, making her wince and icing the sweat stained into her clothes. She laughed, the painful tears now of joy as she gazed upon this great world in new light. She had flown in a plane before, but this was something totally new. It was as though she were free, like a bird, laughing at gravity as it tried to drag her back down to earth.

She was flying!

And all too soon it was over. From the corner of her eye, Angela saw the rope ladder drop down from above. It flapped and flailed in the wind, bouncing about and actually beating against her until Angela finally reached out and got a grip on the rope. She knew that the cameras were rolling, and Sebastian was waiting. She had to start climbing and finish the shot.

Angela hooked one of the wooden slats with her foot, pulling the ladder closer until both feet were resting on the wood. She took a firm grip on the rope and unhooked her arm from the axle, immediately groping for the ladder as she shifted her weight.

Something snapped!

Angela gasped as one of the ropes holding the ladder together broke. The ladder swung wildly sideways, off balance because of her sudden weight and caught in the grip of the wind. Angela struggled to hang on, trying to right herself as she groped blindly, trying to grab the axle once again. She stretched, whimpering, praying as her fingers brushed the leather wrappings about the hot metal. There was a sudden jerk.

And she was falling.

Angela screamed!

❀ ❀ ❀

EPISODE SIX:
THE LAIR OF THE CAT!

El Gato Negra watched with rapt attention as the girl started running, cheering with the rest. The flying machine- the aeroplane bore down on her like some great bird of legend, its vast wings outstretched, cawing and screaming and spitting smoke. It was incredible! El Gato Negra had never seen the like in all her years in the Green.

The girl, Angela Morgan, was strong, and not afraid. Selia- El Gato Negra, High Priestess of the People respected her for that. Selia even felt the slightest guilt that one so brave should have to die, but the People, and the Green had to be protected. She had seen the girl survive leaps and falls that would have vexed many of her clan of the Jaguar Cult. The girl had survived the Breath of the Viper, and escaped death at the claws of the Avatar of the Nekara. Now she was running from the flying machine, and if Selia understood the strange customs of the Blancas, she would latch on to the belly of the beast and then climb up and in. To safety, or so she thought at least.

But Selia had watched and listened, and learned. It was simple enough, wearing the face of the older woman, Gloria Swann, whom she had captured almost three days before. Using the ancient sacred masks, El Gato Negra had stolen the woman's face and memories and taken her place amongst the Blancas; the ancient arcane magick turning her brown skin to a lighter shade of tan that allowed her to pass for white. They had accepted her readily; the magicks of the masks also let her speak their vile

"Angela screamed!"

tongue with ease and tell them the lies that they would believe. Selia had worked her way into their midst, pretending to be the woman, looking for some way to route them and send them away.

She had seen the aeroplane, the great flying machine and thought that the Gods of old had returned to seek their vengeance. The outsiders however had been unaffected by the appearance of the sky beast, and some had actually waved to it, smiling. Selia was astounded to see it wave back, not only its great dipping wings, but also another within the belly of the mammoth bird. The great beast it seemed was just a machine after all, carrying a man, old and used. Still, Selia had run on ahead of the others to see the machine, to watch it come to earth and investigate its abilities. The old man within had been annoyed, as Selia had babbled like a child, but he answered her questions and showed her things; some that confused her, and others that she understood.

She had pestered the old man with her eager questions until he had left in exasperation, excusing himself to go to something called a 'latrine' with a promise from her that she would not touch anything until his return. She had lied of course, as, as she truly had been marveling at the flying machine and its wonders she had noticed the rope ladder that would be used in the stunt later and a plan had formed swiftly in her cunning mind. She had quietly waited eyeing the camp and its people as she slipped a slim knife from the pocket of the captive woman's stolen clothes. And as quietly, she had slit the ropes that held together the ladder that the girl would climb later that day. Not enough to sever the links, but enough that the rope would not support the girl's weight. If Selia understood, the girl would be hanging from the flying machine, trying to climb within using the ladder. The ropes would snap and she would fall, regrettably to her death. It would be enough, however, and the invaders would leave, and the Green would return to normal at last.

So El Gato Negra had watched as the girl ran, stumbling as she groped and finally reached the wheels of the machine as it swooped in low. Selia cheered with the rest; it was amazing and she felt her heart beating madly caught up in the excitement. The girl dangled as the aeroplane swooped up and away, gliding softly on the wind. Selia found herself gasping with the rest as the girl groped for the rope ladder flapping in the breeze almost within reach. She cheered when Angela finally grabbed hold. She tried not to cheer when the ladder broke away and the girl started to fall.

There were screams, and almost as one the crowd surged forward, watching as Angela kicked and flailed as she fell. Selia had hoped that the

girl would hit the top of the plateau and end it all quickly, but all too soon
her body vanished, dropping beyond the edge of the mesa. Selia cursed
softly as she ran along with the rest, right up to the ledge, though she
knew what she would see. The Green stretched out before them, the vast
canopy of the jungle rolling away as far as the eye could see. The girl had
disappeared into the jungle, her passage lost and ignored save for a flock
of birds on the wing at the sudden disturbance.

The girl was dead, and soon the outsiders would leave. They would
search, of course, and the jungle might even give up its dead, eventually,
but their time here was finally over. Selia bit her cheek, trying not to smile.

Gloria Swann sagged in her bonds, exhausted and full of self-pity.

She had lost track of the days that she had been held prisoner- four…
five? She did not know. All that she knew was that she was miserable. She
was filthy, hungry and thirsty and she was tired of being tied up.

The cavern that her three captors were keeping her in was huge and
dimly lit, with a scattering of torches barely illuminating the walls.
Sunlight beamed in from somewhere high above, but it did little to cut the
gloom and it never seemed to move, simply winking out at times for short
intervals that could not have been a full night. Water dripped, echoing
in the distance in a steady rhythm, but Gloria was too weak and tired to
focus on it for long. The monotonous dripping seemed to lull her into a
dull daze rather than keep her attentive and focused besides.

Gloria sighed, rotating her wrists again in the coils of rope looped
behind her back. She had been trying to gain her freedom forever it seemed,
but was actually getting nowhere. She had been re-tied to the wooden pillar
where her captors had originally bound her, finally allowing her enough
slack to sit down. They had stretched her arms back and behind the totem
pole, lashing her wrists tightly. She was sitting with her back to the pole,
her legs crossed at the ankles and bound as well. She was still gagged too,
a long strip of leather tied tightly about her head, forcing her teeth apart
and holding in a ripped and balled up bit of cloth from her own clothes.
The gag hurt cutting into her cheeks and soaking up her saliva. She could
not swallow or talk and she could barely move. Gloria twisted her wrists,
pulling at the coarse ropes, wishing herself to freedom that would not
come.

It was humiliating as well sitting there, hour after hour, totally helpless
and dependant upon her captors. She watched them, the two women
remaining who held her captive, sitting on rocks on the far side of the

cavern. They were still dressed almost like the women that made up the extras in her movie; animal skins and leathers for the most part, though they wore some gold and silver jewelry as well. They were beautiful, in a savage sort of way, with long tanned legs and incredibly statuesque bosoms. They were tall as well, both well over Gloria's own five and a half feet, and probably over six. Their hair was wild and in dirty disarray, but thick and lustrous as well. Gloria would have wrecked careers to have hair like that. Gloria felt inadequate in their presence, and worse, humiliated as she was dressed only in her smalls; her dirty, sweat-stained brassiere and silken slip.

For all her titles and bravado she was trapped and helpless. The leader of the trio, the most exotically beautiful of the Amazons had had her tied to the totem pole in their secret cavern hideout. It was a temple of sorts. At least it appeared to be, complete with a bloodstained altar stone. Archaic weapons, pottery and trinkets were scattered about the cave in haphazard disarray. The pole that she had been tied to was a carved totem; images of strange creatures etched into the hard wood capped with the visage of a giant dark cat. The most frightful thing in the cavern however, beyond the squealing rats she saw scurrying through the darkness, and even the Amazons themselves, was the gargantuan carved image of their idol. It was a figure of a man chiseled from shiny black stone, like obsidian. It was huge, towering almost twelve feet, and amply muscled and well endowed. Worst of all was the fearful, snarling face of the panther that it wore. It was like some twisted version of Bast- the Egyptian cat goddess. Gloria wondered if there was some connection in the Amazon's past.

She wondered too what the leader of the Amazons was doing with her face. Gloria had never been one to believe in magic; at least beyond the magic of the movies. Of course, there were the strange occurrences in the Caribbean, and there were places like Stonehenge and Ayers Rock in Australia. Gloria herself had seen the likes of Houdini and Svengali perform seeming miracles as well, so perhaps she should not jump to any conclusions concerning magic. Still, she felt that there must have been some trick to whatever the Amazon had done to steal Gloria's face. Simple enough to make something glow here in the dim cave with the flickering torches and a bit of lichen. There were probably hallucinogens in the smoke filled chamber; in the torches or the incense maybe, or perhaps they simply drugged her with marijuana or peyote. There had been a bit of disorientation, her senses had reeled and she had seen things that seemed like memories but must have been hallucinations ala the Amazon wearing her face.

Gloria had awakened, rebound to the totem pole and nearly naked. The golden masks, shaped like cat's faces, hung from a spear propped up against the great slab of stone that was the altar. The leader had apparently left with Gloria's face and clothes, and it did not take an Einstein to savvy that she was going to infiltrate the film company as Gloria!

The question was, why? Gloria had nothing to do but work at her ropes, however, and think, and eventually all the pieces started to fall into place. All the strange things that had happened on the film shoot, the long string of accidents and bad luck! There was the animal attack on the camp. The bout of sickness that had afflicted so many of the crew that first week caused from the oddly spoiled food. The strange incident near the cliff over the water falls where two stray arrows had almost skewered Gloria. And of course the 'accidents' that had almost killed her stunt double, Angela Morgan. It all made sense. These Amazons were behind everything, all of the troubles that had plagued the film since they had settled in the jungle. But again, the question came up why? Why did the Amazons hate them so? And why go to all the sneaky trouble of making everything appear to be an accident? Why not simply slaughter the cast and crew outright? It almost seemed as though the women would rather drive them away than slay them. Try as she might, Gloria could not find the answer to that one.

So Gloria sat, bound and gagged in her underwear and worked at her bonds. Her captors left her alone for the most part, almost ignoring her. They had fed her a few times, offering some minty tasting pasty mush that Gloria had eaten with a wrinkled nose. She had had to suck it from the fingertips of one of her smirking captors as they refused to untie her for any reason. It was humiliating, but Gloria knew that she had to eat to keep up her strength. They had given her sips of brackish tasting water as well, and quickly re-gagged her, roughly she might add, so as not to hear her complaints. They left her to fend for herself in all other things, which Gloria was not happy about, but there was nothing to do. Nature's call eventually beat her willpower, and Gloria soon found her little area of captivity even smaller. It was another humiliation she had to try and ignore, and endure.

The dull, tedious minutes slowly ticked by, turning to hours. Gloria dozed off and on, as did her captors. She woke once to find one of the remaining pair gone, the other scraping her long knife across a chunk of coarse rock, like a natural whetstone. Of course, Gloria redoubled her efforts to free her bound wrists, sensing that the odds of her escape were almost even, but the other warrior woman returned before Gloria had made any headway on her bonds at all. She was carrying a bunch of bananas and their water skins full to bulging. There was also a long, limp snake draped about her shoulders. Gloria shuddered as the women laughed and settled in, skinning then cooking the snake. When they eventually ate the thing Gloria felt her stomach churning and had to look away.

It was as Gloria was shifting her position after relieving herself that she thought she might have finally found an out. The wood of the totem seemed ancient, almost petrified it felt so dense. The carvings that ran up and down its tall length were chiseled deeply with sharp angles only slightly worn by time. Sharp angles that snagged and chaffed at her skin, and the ropes. Gloria could not seem to work the knots of her bonds loose, though she could not understand why, with all of her experience at escape, but she could saw away at the coarse rope, hoping to eventually cut through. It was her last chance.

Angela Morgan woke in a daze. Her entire body ached; every muscle, every bone. Her hair hurt. She tried to sit up, but her throbbing head started to spin and she felt herself slipping away into unconsciousness once more. She lay back, breathing deeply, waiting for her body to adjust.

It was dark, wherever she was, save for a shaft of golden light beaming down from above. It appeared to be some a cave, some vast, empty cavern that stretched high overhead at least twenty feet above her to the crest of its domed ceiling. The beam of light made it hard to see about her, but if the dust and insects swirling in the sunlight was any indication, the air was not only dark but thick as well. At least it was cool, and despite her aching body, somewhat restful.

As she lay there recovering Angela's thoughts drifted back, trying to recall how she had come to be lying in a prickly matting of dried grass and branches within some dank cave. She had managed the stunt, or most of it anyway, she knew. All too soon however she remembered the rope ladder snapping and her falling.

Angela Morgan had screamed as she tumbled down through the sky. She had no idea how far up she was, or how far she had to fall, but she was sure that she was falling to her death. It was strange, terrifying and yet oddly exciting. One moment her world was blue, the next it was green as Angela tumbled end over end. The wind was wicked and burned at her skin, though she felt cold, oddly. The sun was blazing brightly, exploding in flashes as she spiraled down, blotting her sight with blurry, glowing dots.

She had tried to concentrate and push the fear away, as she saw the ground racing up at her. She had become tangled in the rope ladder, and it took her a moment to extricate herself letting it fly away fluttering in her wake. Time seemed to have slowed as Angela twisted about, kicking her legs and flailing her arms. She spread her body wide, arms and legs akimbo, her clothes flapping in the wind as she fell, the stage ropes still looped about her wrists streaming behind. She could not feel that she had reduced her speed at all, but she remembered from school that if she presented herself in the widest position possible, the laws of physics would take over.

She had stared frantically about, realizing suddenly that she had yet to give up. She saw the river far in the distance, snaking away towards the horizon. There was also a lake, but both were far too far away to help her. Her only hope was that she would die a quick death on impact when she crashed down into the tangled jungle foliage.

Angela watched in mounting terror as the green got closer and closer with every passing moment. Her heart was hammering in her chest, echoing in her ears. She felt suddenly numb all over.

As she stared, squinting into the wind and gritting her teeth she started to see details. The canopy of the green became the tops of the trees littered with leaves and branches that grew bigger and closer every second. She tried to draw breath, but gasped instead as she curled into a ball at the last possible instant. She smashed through the canopy, plowing through the upper branches like a wrecking ball. She heard the cracking of wood, the screams of the startled animals in the treetops as she splayed her body again, quickly, praying that she would not impale herself on a stray branch.

She groped blindly, grasping at anything that hit her hands. Leaves ripped away and the lesser branches that lined the treetops snapped under her sudden weight. Still, her body jerked and bounced. She felt her shoulder pop as she slammed into a heavy branch, and the pain almost knocked her out. Her legs slammed against another stout branch and spun her about. She rammed into another and felt her shoulder pop again, back. She was flailing madly, tumbling battered and bruised.

She hit the ground on her back and felt the air rush from her lungs with a mighty 'whoosh'. Oddly, the expected impact was not as solid and final as Angela had expected. The ground seemed to give way beneath her, and Angela had heard the snapping of wood again, and her fall unexpectedly continued. The dim green was suddenly replaced by darkness as Angela fell, gasping for breath. She had slammed hard then, suddenly. Her body bounced as stars exploded in her vision for a brief moment, right before everything had gone black.

Angela had survived. She had escaped death once again, whether by luck, skill or the grace of God she did not know, but she was alive. Her body ached in places she did not even know she had, muscles she had never used, and bones that she did not know existed. She tried to sit up once again, and made it, though her head still swirled a bit and she had to brace her weight on her arms. Her back ached even more from the effort, and as she probed her body she felt blood at her brow and caking her hair. Carol would be furious, she was sure.

Angela sat there in the dim light for some time, though just how long she had no idea. She ran her hands over her body again and again, more thoroughly, probing for broken bones and was surprised to find none though her skin was gashed and full of bleeding scratches and scrapes. There were no pains that seemed outstanding though, no cracked ribs or snapped vertebrae. Just the aching lump on the back of her head, the bruises on her arms, legs and shoulder. She was incredibly relieved that she had not broken her back, though she was afraid she might be concussed. To her it would have been a fate worse than death to be crippled or paralyzed, not to mention lost in the jungle. She tried to get her legs under her, but ended up slowly rolling and rising from her hands and knees in the end. It was easier, and did not make her head swim so much. She knelt, then eventually crouched, then slowly, shakily stood.

Her body felt weak and nauseous, and her muscles quivered as she stood. She almost fell, and staggered through the darkness as she groped blindly for a wall or rock for support. Her legs and arms worked, albeit sluggishly, and slowly she managed to take a few tentative steps. She ached, her muscles screaming in protest at the effort, but she was walking. Her heart was beating. She was alive and that was all that mattered at the moment.

Angela Morgan plopped down with a sigh of relief onto a smooth, round rock that she came upon in the darkness. Overhead through the hole that she had crashed through she could see the thickening light as night slowly draped itself across the jungle. She tried to survey her surroundings as best she could, while she could. She was in a cave that was thankfully cool and damp. How big she could not really judge, but large she thought. Just at the edge of the darkness she could make out a passage that seemed to go back deeper- a cave within the cave. Beyond that, the cavern seemed round more or less. The opening in the roof seemed almost circular, the edges littered with broken branches and the remnants of ripped and tattered leaves and vines. It seemed strange, and oddly familiar, and all at once Angela realized why.

It was a trap. Like the pitfall that she had fallen into that contained the panther, someone had dug a hole through the ground exposing the cavern below. They had then covered the hole with branches and leaves, hoping that someone might fall in and break their neck. Angela's mind boggled at the odds it must have taken for her to fall from the sky and land on that particular spot. Not that she was complaining, as the camouflage covering the hole had been just enough to slow her descent and to break her fall. She had been knocked out by the impact, true, and her body ached worse than it ever had before, but she had no broken bones and she was not spitting blood. She had survived.

She was alive!

She was, however, trapped. The hole in the roof was far out of her reach, and though she could not see the walls, she suspected that she could not climb them to reach it. She could wait, as she was sure that the others were searching for her, but she had no idea how long, if ever, it might take for her to be found. The Brazilian jungle was huge, and most of it unexplored.

There was the tunnel though. When Angela felt her strength return, and her head had stopped spinning she left the security of her rock and staggered towards the hole in the wall. It was dark within, the last fading rays of sunlight doing little to nothing to light her way. She could imagine all the creatures living there as well; rats and snakes and poisonous spiders that loved the darkness, spinning their webs. There was a breeze however, just a thin gust of wind blowing down from the hole in the roof and whistling down into the corridor. There was an opening somewhere then, though maybe miles away. She had a way out, maybe.

Or she could wait for help that might never come.

Angela stumbled into the darkness, her right hand groping along the slick wall for support and guidance. There really was no choice at all.

Gloria's muscles throbbed with the effort, hours spent rubbing her arms up and down trying to saw through the ropes that held her fast. She felt a little give in the rough cords, the slightest bit of slack and that hope was the only reason she was able to continue. As she rubbed the rope along the edges of the totem her fingers still picked at the knots, her arms strained to pull the ropes apart. She would not be beaten by a bunch of illiterate savages, or she was not Gloria Swann!

She did not know if it was night or day, but her captors seemed to be resting. One in fact was stretched out on the rough, gravelly floor of the cavern, lying on a wide animal skin blanket. The other was sitting with her back against a large rock, but Gloria could see that the Amazon was bored. Her head drooped and nodded as she tried to stay awake. Gloria knew that it would not be long before she drifted off to sleep like her fellow.

Finally, Gloria felt the rope binding her wrists start to fray and unravel. Her fingers started picking at the strands, and all at once they seemed to come apart, untwisting with the simplest actions of plucking and pulling. She felt the bonds pull apart with slack, and the ropes loosened, loops rolling from her wrists. Gloria rotated her wrists, gaining inches, and suddenly she was free.

She started to moan as she moved, then quickly stifled the sound, glancing at her captors. Neither stirred, and the one that was supposed to be watching her was asleep, her chin resting on her chest, her head lolling. It was ecstasy to be able to move her arms again, but Gloria knew she had to do so slowly. Her body was still bound, and she needed to free her legs and torso before her captors woke up and put the kibosh on her plans. She eased her arms in front of her, watching the women all the while. The one on the ground was snoring, which disguised Gloria's movements, but kept the other warrior on the edge of waking. She drew her legs up against her breasts, reaching forward to let her fingers dance across the bonds wrapped tightly about her crossed ankles.

Even in the dim flickering torchlight, now that she could see the knots it was child's play to free herself. Her eyes picked the knots apart, her hands mimicking the movements in her mind and within seconds she was uncoiling the loops that held her ankles together. A simple matter then, to remove the ropes at her throat and torso, and finally move on to that damnable gag.

Gloria sat back against the totem, unknotting her gag and stifling the desire to break and run. Her hands and feet were tingling with pain as blood rushed back into them, and Gloria knew that she must wait lest she try to go too soon and fall flat on her face. She massaged her wrists and rubbed her bare legs together trying to bring some life back into her appendages. All the while she watched her dozing captors, but they remained oblivious to what she was doing, dreaming whatever warriors dreamed.

After some time Gloria decided that she was as ready as she would ever be. She was hot, stinking and sweaty, tired and aching, hungry and thirsty, and above all scared. Gloria Swann was terrified that she would be discovered and recaptured, bound and gagged and forgotten with the Amazon leader taking her place in the world. She feared she would be killed. She did not want to die.

Gloria rolled over onto her hands and knees, gritting her teeth and trying to ignore the pain as sharp rocks and gravel dug into her bare knees and the palms of her hands. She wanted desperately to crawl towards the side tunnel that the Amazons had been using to come and go, but that path would lead her directly past her captors, within just a few feet. There were other tunnels however, and she prayed that one of those would lead her to freedom. Swiftly and silently then she crawled on all fours for the closest, well away from the slumbering Amazons.

The darkness of the passage swiftly enveloped her and what little sight she had left her. She was blind, but crawled on, picking up speed, trying to ignore what might lay ahead. She pictured animals leaping out at her; tigers and snakes, spiders! God, she hated spiders.

Gloria struggled to her feet and started to run at a jogging pace. She trailed her right hand along the wall as a guide with her left out and up in front of her, racing along as fast as she dared, not wanting to slam into a wall or a stalactite hanging from the ceiling. She feared tripping and falling, breaking a leg or twisting an ankle at the least. She was terrified that she might fall off a ledge or down a hole and become trapped or injured, dying in the darkness, a long, lingering death with two broken legs, hopeless and alone. The tunnel turned and she ran on following the curve more fearful of being recaptured than anything else. There seemed to be a weak glow in the distance, but she never seemed to draw any closer.

She could see in places, faded patches of greenish gray rock that felt slimy to touch and glowing faintly with some strange lichen or moss. Somewhere in the distance she could hear water rushing, the echo of some forgotten, underground river. It was cold in the tunnel. She felt things, slimy and sticky on the walls and Gloria found that she was soon crying in desperation, wanting to escape this new hell.

Gloria screamed as the ground crumbled and gave way beneath her feet. Her arms windmilled wildly as she kicked her legs trying to run on thin air. She groped blindly, trying to stay aloft, trying to grab anything that might stay her impending fall. She did not know how far above the floor she might be, but even a drop of a few feet might prove fatal if she landed unprepared.

She slammed into another ledge, hitting her in the belly and forcing the air out of her lungs. Her arms shot forward, her fingers digging into the hard, rocky dirt trying to find purchase. Her nails scraped along the ground as gravity pulled at her legs, her weight trying to drag her down. The ledge scraped at her stomach, her bosom, finally her arms as she slipped deeper, falling.

Finally she came to a stop, her fingers hooked over the edge of the trail above her. Her legs scrabbled along the cliff face as she tried to find a toehold to ease the strain on her fingers, but the walls were smooth and slick and far too sheer. She was out of breath, and fear gripped her heart sending shivers up and down her body. She tried to pull herself up, but she just did not have the strength and all too soon she felt the ground starting to crumble beneath her fingers from her efforts.

Gloria sagged, clutching at the ledge as best she could, holding still. Her already abused muscles screamed their protest sending waves of pain through her ravaged body. She took deep breaths, trying to regain what little strength that she could muster, trying to ignore the pain and the sweat stinging her eyes.

She could hear the river clearly now, and a cool breeze licked at her bare feet and legs, blowing up and under her thin silky slip. She chanced a glance down, immediately regretting the action. There was some natural illumination at work, and far below Gloria could see water sparkling and swirling in the queer light. She had no idea just how high up she was, but she was certain that it was a longer drop than she could survive. She saw no convenient ledge or vine that she might grab. There was nothing but cold, hard, smooth rock.

Gloria tried not to cry as she adjusted her grip. Her hands were sweating, and she felt that her fingers were going to snap off from the strain of supporting her weight. Again she tried to find a grip with her toes, hoping to relieve the strain and pull herself up. She actually gained a few inches before slipping down again, the ground of the ledge above too hard to get a solid grip, or really dig her fingers in. She whimpered in frustration.

Gloria screamed as something pressed down on the fingers of her right hand. The pain was intense, as though her fingers were being crushed by a massive weight. She lost her grip in the pain, feeling the ledge crumble in her fingers with the added weight. Oddly, it felt as though someone had stepped on her hand, as the pressure was soft, like the sole of a boot. Gloria screamed again, realizing that she was going to fall to her death. Her captors had found her again, and this was her punishment for trying to escape. They were killing her, grinding down and trampling on her fingers until she finally fell.

The sudden weight lifted, too little too late. Gloria hung precariously by one hand for a heartbeat, her fingers slipping even as the rocky ledge crumbled and broke away in her grip. She looked up to see a shadowy form staring back at her, then Gloria Swann started to fall.

❀ ❀ ❀

EPISODE SEVEN:
A DARK PASSAGE!

Gloria Swann let out a little yelp that was half pain, half fright as her already abused fingers scratched desperately at the slick rock wall before her, trying to find new purchase. There was none.

She had been so close.

Gloria screamed, falling away from the ledge. Frantically she started kicking and grabbing at empty air as gravity tried to drag her down. There was nothing to break her fall. Nothing to catch her but the river far below no doubt littered with jagged rocks and racing rapids that would drown her even if she survived the fall. She was doomed.

Something suddenly clamped about her arm and Gloria stopped abruptly short, her plunge barely begun. She swung, slamming against the wall with enough force to rattle her teeth and bloody her knees. She felt her shoulder pop, and immediately felt a new pain race through her outstretched arm. She heard a grunt from above and realized that someone must have grabbed her forearm, preventing her from falling to her death. Gloria felt herself slipping though as if whoever was hanging onto her was having a hard time of it. Her body fell a bit, and she felt fingers digging into her skin with enough force to bruise and draw blood. The hand about her arm slipped down to her wrist slick with sweat. Gloria stretched, straining to reach up and latch onto her rescuer's arm in return, but she hurt too bad, was too tired. She groped pathetically at empty air, out of reach.

She dropped a bit more, sliding against the slick face of rock a few more inches and felt another hand lock about her wrist below the first. Her shoulder was throbbing from the pain, the strain of her own weight. Her fingers tingled, growing numb.

"Damn it, Gloria! Help me!"

Gloria Swann gasped; blinking at the sound of the raspy voice that had called out her name. It was a voice she recognized, though it was strained and weary from the effort of holding her.

"Ang…" she choked, having not really spoken for several days. Her own voice was raspy as well, and her throat sore from the sudden unfamiliar effort. "Angela?" she finally managed from her burning throat and chapped lips.

"Yes!" the voice cried with a shrill sob.

It was Angela Morgan, her stunt double from the movie. Gloria could not begin to fathom why the girl was there in the caves, nor why she was even helping her. Gloria knew that she had given none of the cast or crew reason to like her, let alone risk their lives for her. Especially Angela! They must have been searching for her all along she thought.

"Jesus, Gloria! Climb!" she heard Angela scream through gritted teeth. Gloria could feel the girl's grip slipping, losing hold of her sweaty arm. "You're too heavy! I can't hold you!"

"Oh, god!" Gloria whimpered. She did not want to die. She tried to pull herself up, but she was too weak and out of shape. She could brush her fingertips over Angela's arm, but could not get a grip. "I… I can't…"

"You can, Gloria!" Angela cursed, and Gloria felt the girl's own perspiration dripping down onto her face. "Swing your leg up. Try to find a foot hold!"

"I can't!" Gloria whined, crying. It was getting hard to see, harder as her eyes welled with tears.

"You better! So help me god, Gloria, I'm not going with you over the edge! You help me or I drop you! Do it!"

Gloria sobbed, but she could hear the edge of steel in Angela's voice. She was serious. She would let Gloria drop if the star did not try to help save herself. Gloria gasped, biting down on her lip as she scrambled, her legs kicking and scurrying, trying to find a toe hold on the slick, slimy surface of the rock face. She slipped again and again and felt her skin scraping and bleeding before long. Her toe nails cracked and split, bending back and sending new, excruciating pain through her feet. Gloria started to cry harder, but she did not stop trying.

At last she felt a slight crack that she might be able to slip her toes into. It was just enough to push her body up a bit, and she felt Angela's hands rotate, getting a better grip.

"That's it. More, Gloria! Swing your leg up higher!"

Gloria grunted with the effort, kicking up with her other leg. She had not had to lift her legs so high since she had been an extra in a chorus line on Broadway. It hurt, and she felt bones popping in her legs. Her muscles cramped up in her thighs and calves, and Gloria winced, trying to ignore the agony. With a mighty effort she hooked her heel onto the crumbling ledge.

Gloria gasped when Angela released her left-handed grip and quickly snagged the back of Gloria's brassiere with that free hand. Gloria felt the girl tugging, trying her best to haul her up and over the lip of the ledge. The stiff material of the brassiere cut into Gloria's skin, digging into her armpits and pinching her breasts. Gloria let out a little moan of pain, scrabbling all the harder to heave her bulk up and over the edge. Then suddenly, with a final grunt from both women, Gloria slumped back onto the trail collapsing in a heap.

They lay side by side, Gloria on her stomach, Angela on her back. Both were breathing hard, heaving in the dank humid air. They were exhausted, and both reeking from the effort, smelling of sweat and the unwashed. Gloria wanted nothing more than to surrender to her fatigue and fall asleep right there, but all too soon Angela was talking again.

"Gloria? What happened? What are you doing here?" There was a moment's silence as both women caught their breath, then, "Where are your clothes?"

"Angela!"

Jennifer Higgins cupped her hands around her mouth and screamed her friend's name once again. As before, her call was met by the shouts of the others calling Angela's name, but no response came from the stunt woman herself. She had not really expected Angela to answer though. It had been hours since she had fallen from the biplane and dropped down into the thick, steaming jungle. Even if she had survived, well, she had fallen so far that if she was still alive she had to be unconscious at least, and probably crippled to boot. She was probably unable to answer, even if she was somehow awake.

Jennifer flopped onto a smooth, moss-covered rock and stretched, waiting for the others to catch up to her. She could hear the others that she had coupled with as a search party stomping through the brush not too far away; Alice Simmons, along with Joyce Needler and Ginger Sachs; two more of the eight Amazon extras on the film. Like Jennifer, all three were on the buxom side and leaning towards beautiful, in a leggy sort of way. None of them had any illusion that they had been hired for their acting abilities, but then too, none of them really cared. It was a Gloria Swann

"You're too heavy! I can't hold you!"

vehicle, after all, and it would not win any awards, though it would no doubt make money. Gloria's movies were, rather, adventure serials, and hardly deep, thought provoking films. To Jennifer and the other Amazons, it was a paycheck. In fact, Angela was about the only one of the crew that put her all into her shots every day. To her, this film was like her first, each shot a new experience. Jennifer did not know how she had done it.

Did it!

Jennifer shook her head, trying to clear her thoughts. Angela was not dead. Not yet! Not until they found a body at least. Though that was proving to be an impossible task, dead or alive.

After Angela had fallen, and the initial shock had worn off, almost everyone had run down the trail of the plateau and started searching willy-nilly, charging headlong into the jungle. Karl was the worst, screaming Angela's name over and over, tears streaming down his face. In fact, the only ones who did not seem totally shaken by the catastrophe had been the director, Jonathan Harkins, and Gloria Swann herself. They had come down from the mountain, but Harkins only after he was certain that the film from the day was being stored properly, keeping the cameramen and editors behind. Gloria came down almost sauntering, barely hurrying and staying well to the rear of the group. Karl Braun had rushed madly into the jungle, as would have everyone else had John Thomas, the assistant director, not organized everyone into small groups. Sebastian, the pilot of the biplane had continued flying in circles over the area that he thought Angela might have fallen, but he had been forced to land not long after as the wind had picked up and it was getting too dark for him to stay up in the air.

It was almost too dark to see on the ground as well. The gibbous moon was out providing some light, but clouds were rolling into the area and Jennifer knew too well that before long there would be storms raging across the land again. It was still hot, and humid as well, and the jungle air was thick with insects. Jennifer heard night birds as well, and bats that fed on the insects fluttering through the treetops. She heard the occasional screech of a monkey, but more often the low guttural growl of one of the great jungle cats. She was getting nervous, and sorry as she was for her missing friend, soon they would have to call off the search for the night.

Before long Ginger and Joyce joined her. Jennifer could barely make out their faces in the darkness, and was glad that they had finally caught up with her. She pushed off of the rock, standing to meet them, then looked about curiously.

"Where's Alice?" Jennifer asked, trying to peer back through the jungle along the trail the trio had blazed. Ginger shrugged.

"We figured she was with you, Jenn." The buxom red head sat on the very rock that Jennifer had rested on and began to undo the leather laces of her animal skin leather boot.

"We haven't seen her for awhile now, hon." Joyce sat on the edge of the rock beside Ginger, watching as her friend slipped off her boot and upended it, shaking out some small pebbles. "Maybe she headed back to the camp?" the pretty brunette said, her dark eyes sparkling in the moonlight. Joyce had an exotic, Grecian look to her, with dark, almond eyes that made Jennifer weak in the knees they were so alluring.

"Maybe," Jennifer only half agreed. Alice had been with them, actually lagging as far behind as Jennifer had gone ahead, her fear for Angela giving her an unbridled energy at first. She found it hard to believe that Alice would have abandoned the search, or wandered off on her own without telling one of them first.

"Maybe we should head back?" Ginger suggested as she slipped her foot back into the tiger skin boot, wriggling it into place. She folded her leg up, knee under her chin as she re-laced it. "It's gettin' kind'a dark." Joyce agreed of course, holding her hair up off of her neck, just silhouettes in the dim moonlight.

"I suppose…" Jennifer agreed with a sigh. "I hate to give up, but I guess it wouldn't do any good if we all got lost too. You two head out. I'll bring up the rear. And keep an eye out for Alice, just in case she got lost."

The two women nodded and stood, took a quick look about and swiftly headed back the way they had come. Jennifer stared after them until they vanished into the jungle, still unwilling to give up the ghost. Angela was out there somewhere, and Jennifer hated to leave her maybe hurt, unconscious, even dead and food for some jungle beast. She shivered, trying to force that thought from her head. With a sigh and a sorrowful shrug, she eventually started back as well.

Angela trudged on through the dark tunnels that seemed never to end. She was hot and sweating despite the cool of the caves, and tired beyond belief. She ached everywhere, and with every step a pain stabbed in her ankle. It had started hurting more and more as she had made her way through the underground caverns, though it had not seemed to hurt at all when she had first started out. She suspected that it was sprained, and she knew that if she stopped she would never get going again. So she kept staggering forward, enduring the pain and exhaustion, as well as the constant whining of Gloria Swann coming from behind her.

Angela had been so happy to find a familiar face that at first she did not care why Gloria had been in the tunnels wearing only her smalls. She had been frantic, of course, to find the star dangling from the crumbling ledge and the effort to save her had almost done them both in. It had been worth it, though, for the companionship and the chance that Gloria might know a way out of the dank and confusing catacombs. At least at first.

It became readily apparent however that Gloria was as thoroughly lost as she was herself. She listened as they walked, as Gloria told her the tale of how she had been kidnapped from the shoot and held captive by real Amazons for the last three days and then some. Angela had been impressed by Gloria's story of her escape; how she had slipped free of the ropes that they had bound her with and how she had fought off the two warriors to run down the tunnels for freedom. That was what she knew best of Gloria Swann; the Gloria of old that she had seen every Saturday afternoon in her youth. Gloria Swann was the Queen of Escapes after all.

Angela was a little concerned however, when Gloria said how the leader of the warrior women had used some strange type of mask to disguise herself as the star. If Gloria was right, then the woman that had staggered out of the jungle two days ago had not been Gloria at all, but rather a real Amazon who was apparently the one behind all the misfortunes that had plagued the movie set over the past fortnight. It was all rather bizarre, but with all that had happened over the few weeks that the crew had been in South America, it was almost believable.

Angela told Gloria as well of her own plight; how she survived the fall from the aeroplane, coincidentally falling through the pitfall that probably the Amazons had built over the great cavern where Angela had woken up. Angela figured that it was probably the drop through the thick jungle canopy as well as the break away camouflage over the pit that had actually saved her, the leaves and branches of the latter actually cushioning her fall in the end when she finally crashed to the ground.

The two women compared notes as they walked, but neither was in perfect shape, and Gloria was soon whining at the pace that Angela had set, while the stunt woman was snapping at Gloria who seemed to complain about every little thing. Gloria had taken to hanging on to Angela's shirt tail, letting the younger woman lead the way through the dark tunnels and actually letting her drag Gloria along. Angela could feel when the movie star started to lag behind, and it only slowed her down, as she was dead tired herself and ready to drop.

Worse, they were definitely lost and probably wandering in circles. They had retraced Angela's route when Gloria had said that the two Amazons were probably tracking her, but the further they went, the more Angela was convinced that they were going nowhere. There was nothing that she recognized along their route, and everything looked the same. There was just enough light to see by in the eerie glow of the strange moss lining the cavern walls, barely, but not enough to distinguish one bit of rock wall from the next. The dirt and dust on the cave floor was not deep enough to leave any proper tracks along most of their route, and even if it was, the two of them were kicking it about too much to even try to see where they had passed. Their only option seemed to press on, so Angela steeled her nerves against Gloria's complaining voice and did so.

It was impossible to keep track of the time, but Angela figured that they had been walking for a few hours when she saw a faint light ahead. Despite Gloria's protests, she hurried forward, focusing on a thin beam of light coming from the roof of a vast cavern up ahead, hoping that they had not come full circle to where she had started from. Angela felt a breeze as well, and it seemed that there might be a way out. She was rushing forward when she heard Gloria's plaintive moan.

"Nooo…"

Angela stopped, glancing back at Gloria who seemed to have a look of total defeat on her face. She could hear the woman starting to cry again, causing Angela to look back at the chamber ahead. It was a vast room, stretching high and wide, and in the roof was a hole, far overhead. As her eyes adjusted to the dim light, however, she saw things that Gloria had described before from the chamber where she had been held captive; chests of gold and jeweled trinkets scattered about, archaic weapons hanging from the walls, an altar stone stained with blood and a statue.

"We're back where I started from," Gloria whined, dropping to her butt on the ground in defeat. "We've run around in a big circle, and right back into their temple." Gloria buried her face in her hands and started to wail in despair.

Angela turned, started to crouch to comfort the other woman and get her moving again. As near as she could tell, they were alone in the chamber, and there was probably an obvious exit that the Amazons used. But they had to get moving to find it. They had to get away.

"Gloria…"

Angela heard the whistle of the arrow slicing through the air before she felt the pain. She glanced up, starting to stand when she saw the wooden shaft sticking out of her shoulder, quivering there. Blood drooled from the spot where the shaft pierced her skin. She thought it odd and wondered what was happening.

Angela screamed as the pain flowed through her shoulder and suddenly she was on her back gasping for air. Her arm felt as though it was on fire, and Angela found it hard to think. She had never experienced such pain in her life. She could hear Gloria screaming, and tried to call out to the woman for help, but her words were slurred and fell on deaf ears.

Angela grabbed at the shaft, sending a new pain racing through her arm as it bent to her touch. She knew that she had to get the arrow out, but it hurt too bad to even touch it. She knew she would not be able to snap the wood and force it through the wound. She would need Gloria's help, but the movie star seemed in shock and incomprehensible. Gritting her teeth Angela forced herself to sit up, bracing on her elbows, and immediately saw why.

Across the chamber she saw two women walking their way. Both seemed little more than shadows, but Angela could see that they were obviously wearing skimpy animal skins and leathers, and both were tall and muscular. One carried a spear, while the other held a small bow to which she was nocking another arrow. They seemed harried, and out of breath themselves, and as they passed into the thin light spilling from the ceiling Angela saw anger crackling in their eyes. They stopped there in the circle of light, and as Angela watched, the one with the bow leveled it at her again. Angela watched as the warrior easily drew back on the string. She tried to scramble away, to find cover, but she hurt too badly, the pain in her shoulder and ankle was too much.

Angela's world started to spin, to fade to gray. She saw the woman fire, loosing the arrow.

Gloria screamed!

Jennifer Higgins stopped short, listening. She had been walking back along the tight trail, hurrying to catch up with Ginger and Joyce, and hopefully Alice as well, when she heard something strange off in the dense brush.

It was probably an animal, she thought, there were enough strange noises that were animals out in the jungle to be sure. But what she heard had sounded more like a grunt, a gasp of pain followed by a crash as though someone or something had fallen into a bush. It had sounded all too human to Jennifer, and she was suddenly worried.

She stared into the darkness, glancing about worriedly at the high grass and brush that surrounded her. She could barely see as the moon's light fading in and out with the passing of clouds over head. She listened, but suddenly the jungle seemed deathly silent. All that she heard was the annoying buzz of mosquitoes hovering about her ears. She tried to call out, her voice squeaking and catching in her throat.

"He...hello..."

Jennifer heard something shuffle in the bushes, moving about. She felt a lump of fear rising in her throat, making it hard to breathe. She was shivering, cold, despite the fact that she was sweating bullets. Her heart was hammering wildly.

"Ahh..."

Jennifer gasped, staring wide-eyed into the darkness, seeing monsters in the shifting shadows. Terror gripped her heart and tried to clamp her feet to the ground. Thomas had warned of animals, predators that roamed the jungle at night, and Jennifer was sure that she was about to face one. Something huge and fierce by the sound of it. Jennifer started to inch along the trail, praying to god that she might live to see another day. She quickened her pace.

Jennifer rounded a bend in the trail and froze.

There, just a few yards before her was something, someone blocking the trail. They were crouched down, clawing at the ground, ripping at a mound of earth for some reason. They were snarling, like a cat, and they seemed in a frenzy, so much so that they had not even heard her approach. Jennifer stepped forward, trying to see better, wishing that her heart was not pounding so loud.

The clouds rolled on overhead, and far in the distance Jennifer felt, more than heard, the first faint rumblings of thunder. The trail brightened, cast in an eerie pale glow and Jennifer stopped short again, her mind reeling with what she saw.

Alice Simmons lay on the ground, her eyes staring wide, glinting in the sudden light. There was blood all about, pooling beneath Alice and spattered around the trail; on the leaves and trees, dark splotches in the dirt. There was a gash across Alice's throat, and Jennifer could see blood, thick and steaming, oozing from the wound. Alice's mouth was open, as though she were trying to scream.

Hunkering over the body of her friend was a woman. Jennifer did not recognize her at first, as her face was turned away, but there was something familiar. The woman's hair was dull and gray, but her skin seemed dark, and her body muscular. She wore a long skirt, and a khaki blouse that was darkened in spots, stained with sweat. At first, Jennifer thought that the woman's hands were claws, the way she was digging at the body beneath her, but as the sky cleared and the moonlight grew brighter she saw that instead the woman wore gloves; gloves of black fur with claws laced in. Despite herself, Jennifer gasped, horror gripping her heart, and the woman finally heard her. The woman turned.

It was Gloria Swann!

Jennifer heard strange noises escaping her mouth as she tried to force herself to back away. It was too much. Too much! Her mind was screaming the shrill cries that her throat was too constricted to release. Gloria Swann was crouched over the body of Alice Simmons, ripping at the dead woman's throat. Killing her!

Gloria started to rise, and finally Jennifer got her legs to work. She scrambled backwards, not wanting to turn away from the grisly scene, but wanting to run as fast and as far away as her legs would carry her. Jennifer was moaning with the terror swelling within her, whimpers of fright with every ragged breath she took. She stumbled along, backing away as Gloria started after her, stalking her. Jennifer turned and ran.

Jennifer felt a sharp pain shoot through her ankle and suddenly she was falling. She cried out, finally, though her scream was cut short as she slammed against the hard packed dirt of the trail, the wind whooshing out of her lungs.

She lay there, her ankle throbbing in rhythm to her heartbeat. Her head was spinning madly, sparkles of gray erupting in her sight as she tried to focus. Her breath came in short gasps, when she could gather a breath at all. She glanced back, struggling simply to move, trying to see what had happened. Jennifer saw her foot wrapped up in the clutches of a tree root that had erupted from the ground in the middle of the path and she had stumbled right into it, like a wolf in a steel jawed trap.

Jennifer moaned, trying to free her ankle, tugging on her leg with a frantic strength. She had to get away! She had to escape before Gloria…

Gloria!

Jennifer glanced up to see the woman stalking towards her. There was blood on her face, spattered on her clothes. Her eyes were darkened slits, like a cat's, and they gazed at her hungrily with a cruel coldness like a predator that had just cornered its prey. Jennifer whimpered, struggling all the harder to free her leg. Death was coming for her, like it had for

Alice. Like Angela.

Jennifer gasped as the woman stopped, crouched...

With a loud, sudden snap, Jennifer pulled her leg free breaking the tree's root from the ground.

Like a cat, Gloria snarled and sprang!

❁ ❁ ❁

EPISODE EIGHT:
PANTHER'S RAGE!

Jennifer Higgins screamed her eyes wide with horror as Gloria Swann lunged through the air at her. Time seemed to slow as the old actress leaped her eyes crackling and a fierce, feral snarl twisting her otherwise handsome face in rage. Jennifer wanted to move to get up and run for all that she was worth, but terror had wrapped her in a bear hug pinning her to the ground.

Her heart slammed into her chest as a fearful second ticked by. She was going to die and there was not a thing she could do about it. Her gaze flitted over Alice's cooling body lying not so far away, her friend's eyes gazing blankly skyward and she knew that in seconds, heartbeats, that would be her as well.

Gloria seemed frozen in mid-leap, caught in the space between those heartbeats. Her arms were outstretched, long bloody claws glistening in the dim moonlight. A vicious snarling roar rumbling from her throat, past her lips, a look of pure hatred that made Jennifer scream once more and started time ticking again at full speed.

A shadow stepped between Jennifer and Gloria, and with a blurred speed the extra heard a thump and suddenly the movie star was sprawling to the ground. Jennifer stared wide-eyed; gasping for a breath that would not come, trying to understand what was happening. She saw Gloria shake her head and fluidly spring to a crouch, her face seeming to ripple in the dull moonlight. The shadowy form stepped up to meet Gloria's challenge, and Jennifer saw that it was a man carrying a broken tree limb, wielding it like a club. Jennifer recognized the denim worn by the man, the worn out cowboy boots and the graying hair even from behind.

It was Karl Braun, the stunt coordinator on the film. He had run off into the jungle alone the second that his apprentice, Angela, had fallen from the aeroplane. He had loved Angela in a fatherly sort of way and Jennifer assumed that seeing her fall to her death had been a crushing blow. He had charged off to find Angela by himself, and had been as lost to the others as she was during the search. He had found Jennifer though, luckily and just in the nick of time. Karl swung the makeshift club with all of his might as Gloria suddenly pounced at him, the intruder, her new prey.

Jennifer heard a loud crack and saw the gnarled limb splinter and break as it connected with Gloria Swann's head. Blood flew from the star's mouth and nose as her head snapped abruptly to one side. Her body went sprawling through the air, tumbling across the ground until it slammed up against the trunk of a large tree with a crash. Gloria looked up, her eyes dazed and glassy, her face twisting between pain and anger. Then her eyes seemed to roll back up into her head and the movie star slumped back to the ground, unconscious.

Jennifer sagged, her body trembling as the terror that had gripped her started to drain slowly away. She moaned, aching and suddenly exhausted from her ordeal as fear-stoked adrenaline washed from her. She saw Karl Braun turn and stare at her, still holding the remains of the club he had used to save her life. He was breathing hard, and sweat was running down his red blushing face. He seemed ready to collapse himself as he stepped forward, tossing his weapon to the ground.

"Are you all right, Jennifer?" he asked, kneeling beside her.

Jennifer nodded. "I think so." Jennifer's hands went to her ankle, feeling the bones to see if it was broken. Karl saw this and pushed her hands aside and pulled off her furry boot. He ran his rough hands over the hot, sweaty skin of Jennifer's foot and ankle, pushing and probing. Despite what had just happened moments before, Jennifer giggled, his fingers sending a tingle up her leg. She tried to pull away, realizing that she was too ticklish, but Karl held on a second longer with a sly grin and a look of determination. He then released her foot and stood, apparently satisfied.

"Just twisted, I think. It will be sore, but it is not broken. You were lucky." Karl Braun turned to stare at the crumpled form of Gloria Swann then, and Jennifer could see the confusion on his face.

"I'll say." Jennifer agreed as she slipped her foot back into her animal skin boot. "Lucky for me you came along when you did. Thank you! If not for you, I think Gloria would have killed me, just like poor Alice." Jennifer glanced at her dead friend, still lying on the ground and staring blindly into space. She could see the ground darkening beneath her body as her life's blood drained away, spreading out in a wide pool. Jennifer felt a lump rising in her throat as tears started to blur her vision.

Jennifer cried for her friend as Karl slowly crouched down beside Alice's cooling body. He touched at the wounds, turning Alice's lolling head from side to side and finally closed her eyelids. Then with a frown he stood once more and took off his denim jacket gently draping it over Alice's face. Head hung low he shuffled back to Jennifer's side.

"She is dead, and none too gently." Jennifer could hear the barely suppressed anger in his voice. "Gloria tore her to ribbons, almost like some animal. Or maybe that is what she wanted it to look like." Karl Braun stared back at the covered body for a moment as though trying to get a grip on some elusive thought. "I have known Gloria Swann for years, worked on many of her pictures and taught her much of what she knows. She is an arrogant snob. A bitch, some would say, but also in her way, a friend. I would stake my own life that she is no murderer. This is all very strange."

"You can say that again." Jennifer sniffled, trying to sound brave. Her heartbeat was finally starting to slow back to normal, and her teeth had stopped chattering. She was drained of energy though and graciously accepted Karl's help to her feet when he offered his hand. She winced at the sudden pain in her ankle, testing it with her weight, but it appeared that Karl had been right. It was not broken, just twisted and sore. She grimaced, but stayed on her feet trying to ignore the pain.

"What do you suppose…?"

Jennifer gasped, pointing to the spot where Gloria Swann should have been. The spot that was now empty.

"She's gone!"

Angela Morgan groaned as she tried to move, her shoulder burning in agony as her weight shifted, the wooden shaft piercing her flesh grinding against bone. Blood gushed with her desperate movement, seeping from the wound and soaking her already filthy shirt, trickling down her arm. Pain swept down her arm as well, and she swiftly felt her hand and fingers growing numb and useless. Her vision swirled, and she was as good as deaf with Gloria Swann screaming like a banshee in her ear. She strained, trying to see, to stay conscious as her sight blurred, gray fuzzing about the edges.

Angela glanced blearily at Gloria who was still on her butt beside her on the dirty cavern floor. Gloria Swann was screeching to high heaven, her voice loud and grating but actually keeping Angela awake. The movie star had been through hell, so Angela could not really fault her for going to pieces, but screaming madly was hardly going to help either of them.

She looked back at her assailants, the two Amazons as their forms blurred in the queer light of the cavern through the tears welling in her eyes. Both horrible and beautiful at once, one bore a spear, the other a small bow with an arrow knocked, the string drawn taut. Angela blinked as the arrow was loosed.

Blinked as the other Amazon swiftly spun her spear and knocked the shaft aside in midair. The arrow spiraled off into the darkness with a clatter and Angela heard it shatter, hitting the rock wall of the cavern. She breathed a sigh of relief as she focused on the two women fading in and out of her sight. They were arguing she could see more than hear, the never-ending wails of Gloria Swann drowning out everything else. Angela took advantage of the distraction and raised her hand up to the shaft sticking out of her shoulder.

The pain was like a fire raging beneath her skin at her slightest touch. She moaned, trying her best to grip the long wooden shaft, but the pain was too much and her vision swam. She slumped to the ground, dizzy and weak, her senses reeling. She could hear Gloria screaming, then suddenly she could not. Gloria Swann's wailing seemed to choke off, suddenly dying in her throat. Angela tried to open her eyes, to look up to see what had happened.

Angela opened her eyes to slits and saw the booted feet of one of the Amazons standing right before her. She glanced up the forever-long legs, past the rounded hips and ample bosom, but the woman's face was lost in the shadows. Angela tried to rise, but the warrior woman placed a foot on Angela's arm, pinning her easily to the ground. Her feeble attempts to rise were ignored as Angela felt the woman grab the arrow protruding from her shoulder and give it a sharp twist. Even over her own tortured sobs Angela could hear her tormentor chuckling. Then fire seemed to blaze through her shoulder and Angela screamed to high heaven, wishing it to stop.

A heartbeat later her vision darkened, glaring red then turning to utter black.

Jonathan Harkins chewed on the bit of his cigar, staring at the pages of the script for the Queen of Escapes spread out across the table before him.

He was desperately reading through the script, going over every line, every scene, trying to salvage what was left of the film and see what he might do with most of his major players missing, maybe dead.

He cursed Gloria Swann under his breath. She had only one real shot remaining, the close-up kiss with Adam Kaine. That of course could be filmed anywhere, even back in Hollywood, on a sound stage, but he did need Gloria. It was a close-up after all, and her fans would notice if he changed stars. That would have to wait.

He could work around the missing extras. Higgins and Simmons were good, but not essential. With the six remaining Amazons, Harkins had more than enough bodies for the final scene where the women came rushing out of the jungle yelling and brandishing weapons as Kaine and Swann flew off into the sunset. He would have Pitt fly the aeroplane of course, and from a distance anyone could take Gloria's place in the biplane. He could shoot around the two missing extras with no trouble. True, Higgins had a great set of pins, and Simmons had a rack that would not quit, but Harkins knew that pretty faces were a dime a dozen back in Tinsel Town. If push came to shove, they would not be missed.

Karl Braun however was another story. Granted, the stunts were over for the most part. There was a simple shot of a woman hoisting herself into the seat of the biplane, but he could fudge that, again shooting from a distance. The Morgan girl was a real trooper, and she would be missed too, not only for her skill at stunt work, but because she was a dead ringer for Gloria Swann. Harkins smirked at his little joke, 'dead' ringer, then shuffled through the papers again. He would miss Braun the most.

Karl Braun was the best stunt coordinator in the business, bar none, and Harkins knew it. They had worked together on several films; Shiloh Sundown, Zombie Invaders from Mars, and even on the Green Plague, Gloria Swann's first attempt at real acting. Braun had won an award for that one, and Harkins had been nominated by the Academy for an Oscar, despite the fact that the film had died in the box office. Karl Braun would be missed, but Jonathan Harkins figured that such was fate. It could not be helped, and life went on. It had too!

"Jonathan..."

Harkins shuffled his papers and notes together at the sound of the voice at his tent flap. He stuffed the script into a leather folder and set it aside before assuming a depressed position in his chair; frowning, head hung low and arms folded over his chest.

"Come in," he said somberly, not a bad actor himself.

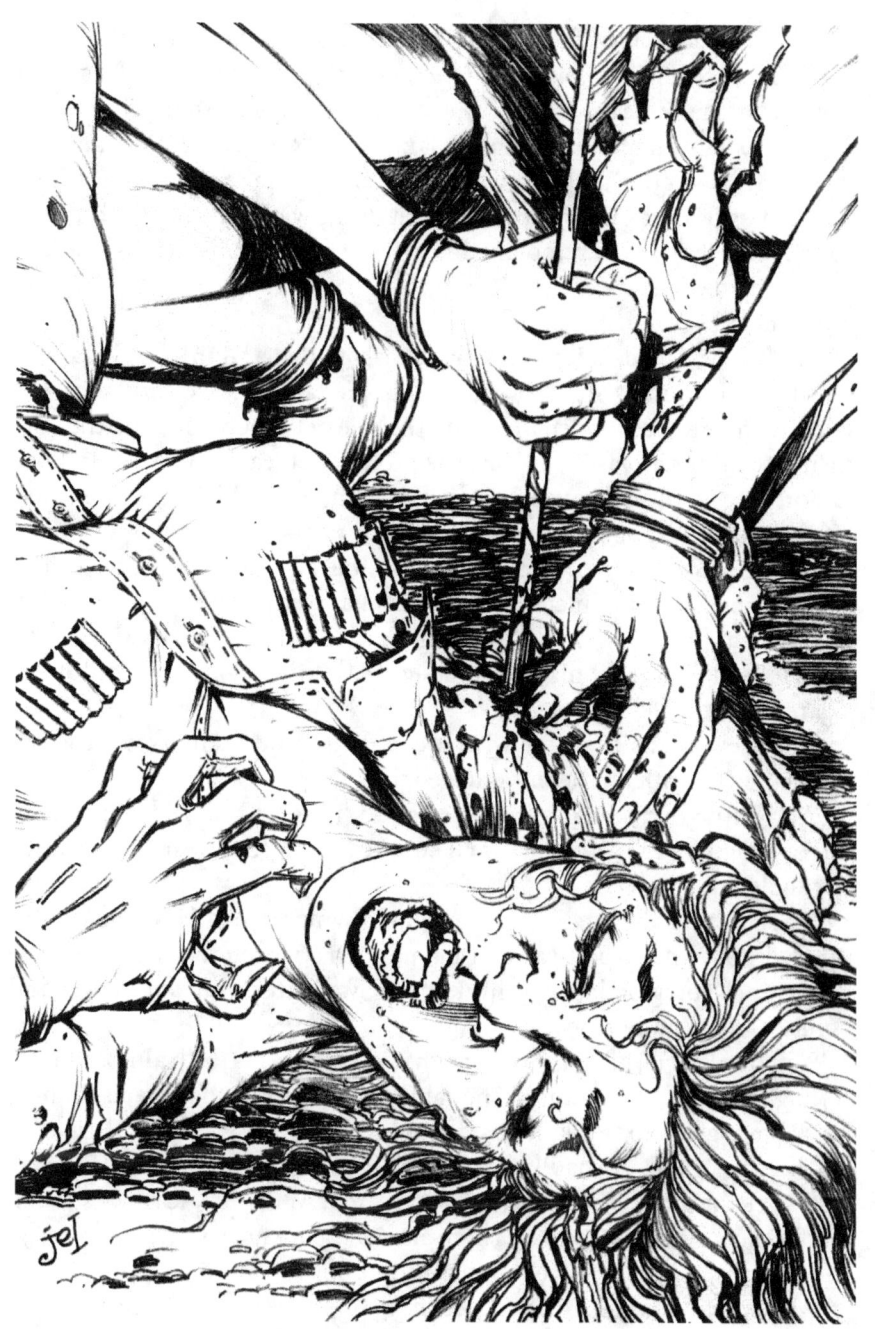

"..Angela felt the woman grab the arrow..."

John Thomas folded the tent flap aside and stepped inside the confines of Harkin's tent. The assistant director on the film was drenched, and Harkins actually heard for the first time the claps of thunder shaking the camp, lightning lighting up the landscape. Rain was falling, another torrential downpour that seemed so frequent in the rain forest. Harkins watched as Thomas shook himself, spattering water about the confined space of the tent before removing his green mac and hat and taking a seat.

"Jonathan…"

"John. What's up?"

Harkins watched as John Thomas slowly pulled a slim, silver cigarette case from his pocket and took out a butt. He tapped the cigarette on his knee, then struck a wooden match on the side of his boot, lighting the butt then returning the case. Thomas was probably at least ten years Harkins' junior, yet the two men were similar in many ways. They had the same height and build. Harkins hair was a bit thinner and grayer, but they both wore it slicked back and short. Still, the toll of years was more readily apparent on Harkin's lined face. Thomas had yet to direct his own film, though that did not seem to bother him, at least as far as Harkins could tell. He settled back as his assistant sighed, taking a long drag off of his cigarette.

"The crew wants to know what we're going to do tomorrow. They're worried, what with all the missing people."

"And with good reason. I'm worried too, I assure you. More than you might imagine. Tell them that we'll keep searching, but we have to get the last shots."

"I don't think they really want to film anymore, Jonathan. Everyone's worried now, and I can't say as I blame them. There's too many bizarre happenings going on lately. I think maybe we better wrap and head back home. Call the authorities."

"You think!" Harkins sat bolt upright in his chair, his teeth almost biting through his cigar. "You think!" he said again, jumping to his feet. "I don't recall paying you to think, John. I pay you to do what I tell you. Period!"

Thomas sighed. He had heard it all before. "I know, Jonathan. But the cast is getting antsy. They're scared. *I'm* scared. At the very least we should send someone back to the base camp and let them know what's happening. They can use the short wave to radio the authorities and…"

"And what?" Harkins snapped, turning on his assistant. "It would take them days to get here, and then what would they do then? Close us down, that's what! You've never dealt with the Federalies, John, but I have. They're a nasty little bunch that does not give a whit about any *Gringos* beyond the color of our money. All's they will do is shut us down and kick us out. Say 'bye-bye' to Gloria, Jennifer, Alice, Karl and Angela, because you will not be seeing them again. South America is the piss hole of the world, John, and the only reason that we're still here is because Gloria greased a lot of palms on our way down. We call in the 'authorities' and it's all over; no film, no rescue, and no paycheck."

"I don't care about the money," Thomas said, sagging as he listened to the director, realizing that he was probably correct. "A lot of us don't. We just want to find Gloria and the rest and get the hell out of here."

Harkins smirked, flopping back into his chair. He knew the man was sincere, and that most of the cast and crew felt the same way. They did not know, however. They had not had to deal with Hollywood and life in general as he had over the years. Most of them had never worked with the likes of Gloria Swann, or the league of lawyers that controlled her assets. They did not have to deal with the company big wigs as he had to. It was all too easy to stick their collective tail between their legs and crawl home. Harkins would be damned before he did that. He was not about to give up.

"Tell you what, John." He smiled, puffing on his cigar, watching his assistant intently. "I'll send the editors back; Walters and his crew, and a couple of hands to guard them in case they're nervous. They can take the wraps with them, everything we've shot so far up here. They can call your authorities on the radio when they get back to base camp. It'll take them a day or so to get back, and a couple days beyond that for the Federalies to get out here. More than enough time for us to wrap up the last of the shooting and to keep searching besides. Hell, for all we know Gloria and the others could come walking back into camp at any moment. Then all of your worries are for nothing."

"Better safe than sorry, Jonathan," Thomas said, standing and donning his rain gear again. It was still storming outside.

"That's right. Better safe than sorry." Harkins stood as well, holding the tent flap for his assistant to depart. "I want the Amazons in costume as soon as the rain lets up after sunrise. And tell Pitt to get his butt in the air too. We have one more flying shot, and we're going to get it as soon as we can. Got it?"

Thomas sighed, shrugging into his rubber mac. "Got it, Jonathan. I'll spread the word." John Thomas tried to smile, but just could not do it. He shrugged finally, then ducked out of the tent and back into the storm.

Harkins let the flap of his tent fall, Thomas and his problems already fading if not forgotten. In his mind's eye he saw the biplane silhouetted against a huge, orange setting sun. On the ground a group of scantily clad women were yelling and shouting at the aeroplane, some of them firing arrows in its wake. The plane would arc out and away, leaving only the setting sun that would eventually fade to black. Then the credits would roll.

Gleefully Harkins opened the folder and thumbed through the pages of the script, making corrections. Damn Gloria Swann, and damn all the rest. He would finish the Queen of Escapes if he had to put on a dress and do it all himself.

Jennifer Higgins had to jog to keep pace with Karl Braun. He was so intent on finding Angela that he had stalked off into the jungle again. Despite Jennifer's pleas he would not slow down, pushing his way through the dense brush.

Jennifer limped along in his wake as best as she was able. Her ankle was throbbing, and it was hard to see so she stumbled along trying to keep the man's back in sight, hoping that she would not fall and hurt herself even more. She could hear the sounds of the animals again, off in the jungle even over the sounds that she made as she thrashed along. She also remembered that 'Gloria' was out there somewhere. Her eyes darted about nervously as she stumbled along, seeing danger in the shifting shadows wherever she looked.

Lightning flared and she yelped as the jungle blazed with sudden garish light. She saw Karl even farther ahead, pale and stark in the swarming shadows of the jungle foliage and soaking wet. Thunder slammed down like a sledge hammer almost knocking her from her feet as she scampered in fright trying desperately to catch up to him. Her eyes darted about nervously, half expecting Gloria to come crashing out of the thick undergrowth to attack her again.

She had been shocked to find that Gloria Swann had vanished. How she had gotten up and away after crashing up against the tree Jennifer did not have a clue. She knew that if she had been hit so hard she would have been crippled for life, if not worse. The woman however had slipped away, apparently dazed only for a short time and unhurt for the most part.

Karl had seemed unconcerned, and after a quick check of the area, he left, giving Jennifer no choice but to follow along or find her way back to the plateau on her own, in the dark. It had taken Jennifer only a moment to make her decision, and soon she was trailing after the stunt coordinator, trying to keep up.

"Karl…" she whined. "Please slow down!"

Jennifer staggered and fell as the trail suddenly sloped down, taking her by surprise. Instinctively she thrust her hands out before her to break her fall, crying out as her palms scraped along the dirt and gravel trail. She banged her knee on a rock, sending a jolt of pain up her leg, then sprawled into a muddy patch at the bottom of the slope. She started to cry.

Jennifer was miserable. She had been hot and sweaty for so long, and then it had started pouring down rain and she had swiftly been soaked to the bone. The rain had been warm and not cleansing at all, and it did little to cool off the humid jungle. If anything the rain made it worse, causing the ground to steam and get soggy and sloppy to walk on. Her animal skin costume had started to smell, and continued to grow worse in the steaming deluge. The ground had become slippery and even muddy in spots and too many times Jennifer had put extra stress on her already sore ankle just trying to maintain her balance. Now she had fallen, splayed face first into a stinking bog of mud. She was covered and filthy, spitting grit from her mouth as she tried to catch her breath. She was tired and sore, and wanted nothing more than to just lay there and rest in the filthy swill.

"Are you all right?"

Jennifer gasped to suddenly hear Karl's rough voice above her. She let out a little gasp of fright, feeling a fool as she looked up to see his shadowy form right before her, leaning down and offering a hand.

"I fell…" she snuffled, feeling stupid as she took his hand. She fought to hold her tears back as Karl easily lifted her to her feet then scooped her up into his arms to carry her out of the bog. She heard his breathing deepen only a little as she draped an arm about his neck to hold on. She wondered where he got the energy to keep going.

After a few steps, Karl gently set Jennifer down at the side of the trail he had blazed, leaning her against a fallen tree, charred and black from an old lightning strike. Jennifer sat gratefully, sighing with relief at the chance to rest. After a few deep breaths she started to use her fingers to scrape the mud from her skin and clothes. She was reeking, the odor almost enough to make her retch, and she wondered if she might have fallen into an animal's nest.

Jennifer heard a familiar sound as she was grooming herself and looked up in time to see Karl flick a smoldering match into the mud, puffing a cigarette to life, shielding it from the rain with his cupped hands. He was waiting for her, she was happy to see, and taking a break himself. Jennifer licked her lips, watching as the cigarette flared while she scraped the mud from her legs, wincing to find a bruise on her knee. She could not see, but she hoped it was not bleeding and worse, getting infected. Jennifer jumped to find the butt of the cigarette thrust before her face.

She glanced up, but Karl's face was blank, and he seemed a million miles away. Jennifer leaned forward, taking the cigarette between her lips and took a long drag while Karl held it steady for her. It was soothing, and Jennifer immediately felt a light-headed rush that relaxed her. She closed her eyes and sighed; blowing out a long cloud of blue-gray smoke that swirled wildly up and away in the storm. She had quit smoking, or tried to, but at times, there was nothing better.

"I'm sorry…"

Jennifer opened her eyes and glanced up at Karl once again. He was looking at her with some concern, his eyes misty and suddenly looking old and alone. He made Jennifer think of her father long dead, and a lump swelled in her throat and chest.

"I should have been watching out for you," he said quietly. "I did not think."

"Karl," she said, surprised as her voice wavered and cracked. "You were worried about Angela. So am I. I understand." A tight grin curled his lips, then just as quickly vanished.

"Still…" He offered her another drag from the cigarette then cast the spent, soggy butt into the muddy bog. He offered her a hand up once again. "Come. I'll take you back to the camp. We will search for Angela along the way, but you should rest. You are hurting."

Jennifer shook her head to deny that, but as she stood pain shot through her ankle again and she was forced to hop forward with Karl's support. She tried to force a smile, Started to apologize…

Jennifer felt the ground sink, giving way under her weight. She gasped as she started to fall back, clutching at Karl's arm as the earth suddenly opened under her feet, collapsing. She saw his eyes grow wide as he clamped onto her arm to hold her, then started to tumble forward as well, caught in the grip of whatever was dragging her down.

"Quicksand!" she yelled, but realized that she was wrong as she kept falling. The ground crumbled, raining down with her. Emptiness opened up beneath her feet.

As the darkness welled up to surround her, Jennifer screamed!

❀ ❀ ❀

Gloria Swann was in Heaven. She had to be.

She had been so tired. She had been aching so badly that she thought she might die. And apparently she had, as now she was at peace. She floated blissfully, her world a soft, comfortable gray that kept her warm and secure. She felt as though she were sleeping, back home in her mansion's bed in Beverly Hills. Soon her maid would slip into her bedroom and draw the curtains, gently waking her for another day. Soon, but for now she was at peace.

Except for the voices.

The voices were rough and loud, chattering incessantly, breaking in on her peace and comfort. She tried to turn away, to bury her head in her pillow, but no matter which way she turned, the voices would not cease. Worse, they were giving her a headache. Gloria moaned in irritation and anger. Whoever was responsible, they would be fired as soon as she woke up.

As soon as she woke up...

Gloria Swann woke with a start, her body jerking in pain as a million muscles seemed to convulse at once. She cried out, but her protests were cut off by something stuffed into her mouth that stifled her noise and breathing as well. Her eyes flew wide, wondering what was happening. Wondering where she was.

Then she remembered.

Gloria Swann was on the ground, shivering despite the heat and humidity. She was all but naked, dressed only in her brassiere and slip, both of which were filthy, stained with sweat and dirt, and even blood. Her hair was a mess, greasy and matted and falling in her eyes, obscuring her vision in the dim that made it even harder to see. Still, she knew immediately where she was.

It was a huge cavern, lit just a bit more brightly than she last recalled. Still she could not see into its farthest shadowy corners, it was so vast. It was a temple she thought again, her sleepy gaze scanning her surroundings once more. The temple of the Amazons who had captured her days before, and apparently had again. She saw the old stone altar stained with dried blood off to her right. She saw the massive statue of the cat man, shining darkly in the torchlight with its jewel green eyes. She saw the crates and chests of golden trinkets, the weapons littering the ground and the decaying tapestry lining one of the rocky walls. She saw the twin carved totem poles and more, and her eyes grew wide in shock.

Angela Morgan stood limply at one of the poles just a few feet away. Her arms were thrust above her head, but the rest of her body seemed to sag, as though about to fall. Her head hung low, lolling forward, her hair hanging in front of her face. Her legs were bent at the knees and Gloria could see that they were not supporting her weight. Gloria stared, straining her eyes in the dim light to understand, and finally saw. Angela's wrists were tightly locked in thick, rusting shackles; manacles that were attached to twin chains that ran to the top of the totem pole where they were no doubt anchored deeply into the wood. Gloria could see a bit of cloth about the girl's lower face, pinning part of her hair in the back where it was knotted, gagging her as well. There was a crude bandage wrapped about her arm also, but even in the thick, smoky light of the cavern Gloria could see that it was filthy and stained dark with blood. She thought the girl must be dead, remembering the arrow, but then she saw Angela's breasts rising and falling rhythmically. Thankfully, the girl was still alive, just unconscious.

Gloria blinked, trying to wish the nightmarish scene away, but every time she slowly opened her eyes again, nothing had changed. Gloria tried to rise, to get up and run away from the Amazon Hall of Horrors, but quickly found that she was just as helpless as her understudy was. Her arms were drawn behind her and, she felt with a quick twisting of her wrists, bound with a thick, rough rope again. She tried to squirm about, lying on her stomach, and found her ankles bound as well. The ropes, coupled with the gag stuffed in her mouth left her helpless and silent, much to her captor's pleasure she was sure.

She saw them then far across the cavern, sitting in the small area of gathered rocks where they had spent most of their time before when Gloria was their prisoner the first time. They were still dressed in animal skin leathers that barely held their statuesque bodies in check. Their hair was still wild and in disarray, and they looked grimy beyond the dark tones of their skin. Still, Gloria was jealous. They were gorgeous. They were talking and at once Gloria knew that they were the source of the voices that she had heard in her sleep. It was some language that sounded almost Spanish, though Gloria could make out no words that she understood. Still, she knew that they must have been talking about her.

Gloria squirmed on the dirt floor, writhing against the ropes that held her bound. She was so out of shape, so out of practice that the effort drained her quickly. It had taken her forever to escape the last time, and it had hurt in the end, chaffing her wrists and straining her muscles. She was in little better shape, if not worse mere hours later, but she felt that the ropes were not quite as tight and thoroughly knotted this time. She felt the slightest glimmer of hope as she struggled, remembering briefly that once upon a time she was one of the greatest Female Escapologists living. She was the Queen of Escapes!

A sudden shouting from the Amazons drew Gloria's attention. She craned her neck, worming back around to see what all the noise was about and quailed. A third person had joined the two Amazons, and Gloria instantly recognized the perfect, muscular body in the khaki clothes even as just a silhouette across the cave. It was their leader; the Amazon Queen!

It was the woman that had stolen Gloria's face. Gloria remembered in horror the glowing golden masques that the woman had used, wearing one and pressing another to Gloria's face. They were cat shaped, and the one burned at the touch. Gloria had been flooded with a wave of images as she donned the golden mask, memories it almost seemed, that were not her own. Gloria had fallen into a daze, but with the last of her strength she had looked up and saw her own face staring back at her. Laughing at her!

The woman, according to Angela, had invaded the set, acting as Gloria to subtly attack and sabotage the film, and probably was the reason for all of their misfortunes throughout their stay in Brazil and the jungle. The Amazon women wanted the film crew gone, out of their jungle for some reason, though Gloria could not fathom the reason why. And, she supposed in the end it did not truly matter.

Gloria watched as the three women argued, the queen waving her arms about and screaming shrilly. A moment later one of the others grabbed up her spear and dashed into one of the shadowy tunnels that pitted the slick rocky walls. The queen then seemed to see Gloria for the first time. She felt the Amazon's sudden, seething rage even from across the cavern and watched as the woman began stalking towards her. Something flashed, glinting in a flare of light suddenly streaming down from the wide hole in the roof as she strode through the glowing circle. It glinted as the woman splashed through a torrent of falling rain falling through the hole as thunder rumbled shaking the cavern. It was a knife!

Gloria Swann squirmed, tugging frantically at her bonds, trying to get away. She started grunting into her gag, trying to wake Angela for help, but the girl remained oblivious to their danger. The queen was almost upon her, coming closer with every long stride. Gloria saw the evil in her eyes, the anger twisting the once beautiful face.

And all at once she knew. Caught in the glow of a torch and the fading light overhead, Gloria saw the twisted, melted flesh once so tight and smooth. Something had happened with the mask. Call it magic, or sorcery, whatever it was, it had gone wrong. The Amazon Queen's face was like a half spent candle dripping away, bleached of color with two black dots where her eyes should have been, a slit that was all that remained of her mouth submerged beneath the baggy flesh. There was a deep dent in the side of her head, as though something had struck her there. Gloria looked on in disgust, revulsion making her want to turn away and retch but fascination holding her, making her stare. It was hideous, made all the worse when the woman snarled, her voice a bone chilling howl.

The woman stopped before her, and Gloria saw the Amazon Queen raise the knife she held high overhead. The woman was going to kill her.

Gloria screamed!

❀   ❀   ❀

EPISODE NINE:
THE FINAL SACRIFICE!

*P*ain!

Selia had never felt such pain before. When the gringo had hit her with the wooden club, she thought that the force of the blow might separate her head from her body. As it was she had been struck senseless, sailing across the clearing and slamming into one of the old, solid trees that filled the Green. She had been dazed, her mind spinning, but worse, she could feel the gift escaping her. The glimmer that had given her the image of the Blanca, Gloria Swann, had been disrupted by the force of the old man's attack, and Selia had felt her face burning as the magicks leeched away, seeping back into the Green.

She had hoped for a fast kill, a quick slashing of her ceremonial claws as she had done on the first woman. She had taken that Blanca by surprise, attacking with the speed and cunning of the jaguar, ripping her throat and slicing until she fell silent. The other woman had surprised her though stumbling upon the kill, and she had been too slow to attack. Then the old man came and she was lost.

She had burned. She could feel her own face melting away as the magic left her, the gift of the Goddess returning whence it came. She wanted to cry out with the pain, but she bit her tongue and remained silent, slinking off to lick her wounds when the pain lessened and the gringos had forgotten her. She had slipped into the shadows, into the cool darkness of the jungle, her home, away to recover. She had gathered her wits, her breath, but she had no time to waste. It was time to drive the outsiders from the land, once and for all before death claimed her.

Selia ran, swiftly and silently like the great cat for which she was named. She was El Gato Negra; the Black Cat. She was sleek and dangerous, the lady of the night, protector of the Green and High Priestess of the Cult of the Jaguar. She would not be bested by these fool outlanders!

She arrived at the cave in moments, the secret tunnel leading into the bowels of Mother Earth, beneath the Green. Her face still burned, and her side was afire; she could feel bones scraping together in her chest with every deep breath, every step. She ignored the pain, or tried to as best she could, struggling to go on. The darkness of the caverns was soothing, comforting as she hurried down deeper into the tunnels. She hoped with all of her heart that Beran and Dyla had the captive in line and prepared. Only the life's blood would satisfy the Goddess now. Only a sacrifice would wake the Guardian to drive the outlanders away.

Selia had entered the Grand Cavern, saw her fellows immediately, relaxing, resting. Fury filled her breast! Her skin burned as anger rushed through her body. Her comrades leapt up as they saw her, gasping in disgust and dismay at the twisted mockery that her face had become. She ignored their fearful, questioning gazes. Their voices fell on deaf ears as she ordered Beran out to find the old man and the girl. Find them quickly and kill them! Beran jumped to the task, eager to be away from the monster that she had become. Dyla hovered about in confusion, and Selia was about to order her out as well when she saw the two captives. Two!

The older one whose memories she still barely shared, Gloria, was still a prisoner, bound and gagged on the dirt floor. What drew her attention though was the other. The one with the very luck of Bel, who she had tried to slay so many times, only to see the woman survive again and again; nine lives like Nekara. Selia strained, trying to grasp the fleeting memories of the older woman, searching for a name; Angela! Beran and Dyla had somehow captured the younger woman and chained her to the Totem of Light. Better still, she was battered and bruised, and unconscious. Excellent!

Selia strode forward, confidence swelling within her again as she pulled the ancient blade from the sheath strapped about her leg. Both women were helpless, bound and gagged and ready for her vengeance; ready to give their lives for the Green that the Mother might survive. Selia's face burned hotter, shame and a scar that she knew somehow would never heal and be her death in the end. Her beauty was gone, but she did not care. She would slay the older woman first and rid her own mind of the queer memories still lingering there. Then she would give the life of the other, so full of energy and the luck of her own brittle brass gods. Surely it would be enough. Surely the Guardian would return.

Selia stood over the Gloria woman and saw the sudden fear in her wide, watery eyes. She was mewling into her gag, trying to squirm away and escape. The older woman knew that her life was forfeit. Selia El Gato Negra raised the ceremonial dagger high. Its panther shaped hilt carved from the same massive black stone as the guardian's statue' a gift from the gods glistening in the flickering light. The two tiny jewels in the handle sparkled, as did the larger eyes of the monument itself. The Guardian smelled the blood, the offering to come. Selia could feel the energy ready to explode from her hands as she held the blade aloft, speaking the ancient words that would call the Guardian of the Green- Nekara, the Panther God!

Gloria Swann stared up at the woman towering above her, straddling her prone and helpless body, waving a long and dangerous black knife high in the air. Her face was a twisted mass of melting flesh; her cheeks and jowls drooping, her dark eyes almost lost in her sagging brows. Her body quivered, almost crackling with excitement of the slaughter to come. Her eyes rolled up into her head as she began mumbling in that guttural grunting that her and the other two Amazon women seemed to speak. Gloria whined and tried to squirm away, tried again to pull at the knots of her bonds, hoping to escape.

She did not want to die like this, captured again; captured by the Amazons. Bound hand and foot and gagged and dumped into the dirt once again like some animal; some pig wallowing and ripe for the slaughter. She was helpless though, but this time she thought that if she had had the time she might have remembered her trade and been able to free herself from the constricting bonds. All that she needed it seemed, was time.

But she knew that her time was at an end.

Angela Morgan shook her head, trying to come awake. She was in pain again, a feeling that seemed to accompany waking more often than not lately. Her shoulder felt as though it was on fire, and dimly she remembered

weight from her swollen, throbbing ankle. She could feel blood running from her shoulder, the wound having reopened from her sudden exertions. The filthy rag that someone had wrapped about the wound was soaked and stained a dark, deepening red. She heard Gloria whimpering again and turned her gaze about.

Angela gasped around her gag; the pains in her battered body suddenly pushed aside by the horror of what she saw. The Queen of the Amazons was struggling to her feet, one of her cohorts helping her; the warrior that had shot Angela with the arrow she thought. What terrified the stunt woman however, was not the women, but the face of the queen herself. Cast in the flickering torchlight it appeared horribly disfigured, twisted and burned, almost looking as though it had melted. Angela could not understand how the woman could see, or even breathe. Her eyes were almost lost in the sagging flesh. She had no nose, and her mouth was little more than a slit in the dripping remains of her skin. Angela saw flashes of bleached white where the hair was starting to fall away, patches that had to be bone! The woman's face was dripping and dissolving even as Angela watched on in mounting horror.

The queen shuddered, her entire body shaking as she tried to find her balance. Angela could only imagine the pain that was attacking the woman, pain that made her own pale in comparison. She watched as the woman shrieked in agony, in anger, shoving her warrior friend aside. The queen staggered forward, and Angela saw that she was going for the knife.

Gloria Swann was stunned when she witnessed Angela Morgan's heroic actions saving her life once again.

She turned back and saw the other Amazon running to help her fallen queen. Gloria had needed time, and thanks to Angela, she suddenly had it. Not much she knew, but it would be enough. Determination swelled in Gloria's breast as her fingers began twisting and groping for the coarse ropes that bound her wrists. They were thick and rough and even the slightest movement hurt and chaffed at her already abused skin. Gloria ignored the pain however, having survived far worse. Her fingers ached, numb and tingling all at once as they danced over the tightly bound cords. The knots were suddenly there, easily within reach. The Amazons had thought her old and spent, easily made helpless. They were wrong.

Gloria traced the knots; simple square knots tied one upon the other. The women had not even bothered to criss-cross the ropes as they bound her, simply looping the cord about her wrists several turns. Gloria's

"She swung about…kicking out with her feet…"

fingernails were jagged and bent back from when she had been hanging from the cliff face before, when Angela had rescued her. Gloria sneered, biting down on the gag in her mouth, furious over how pathetic she had been then, focusing past the pain in her fingers as she picked at the top knot. She stared at the Amazons, watching as the warrior tried to lift the stunned queen to her feet. She felt the rope slip as the first knot opened to her struggles. Carefully but quickly Gloria slid the loosened cord through the hole of the knot, separating the ropes and started probing the second. Gloria resisted the urge to tug on her bonds, knowing that that would simply undo her meticulous work and slow her down. The second knot was looser than the first, and she easily began to thread the tightening cord through the simple web binding her. Though the second knot was not as tightly tied, the trailing ends of the rope were now longer. Sweat was beading on her brow and back, between her breasts making her itch as though she was covered with insects. She grimaced, watching as the Amazon queen pushed her helper away, trying to get her bearings. Gloria saw the tiny beads of her eyes glint in the torchlight and followed the woman's gaze. The knife was lying just a few yards away at the base of the big black stone statue. Gloria cursed as the second knot fell away, but not before the Amazon stumbled towards the blade.

Selia, High Priestess of the Cult of the Jaguar, El Gato Negra, the Black Cat staggered forward. Her mind swam, screaming in agony as she tried to focus on her goal. Her vision was clouded and red from the pain that washed across her face and throughout her body. She was dying, she knew, but she would save the Green with her last efforts. It was her duty, her honor!

Through the smoldering haze of her sight she could see the Swann woman writhing about in terror, knowing that her own end was drawing closer with every failing beat of Selia's heart. The air was thick, and every breath was a struggle, every step a new sensation in agony. The ceremonial dagger seemed miles away rather than a few short feet, but Selia stumbled on.

She slumped against the statue, the great monument of the Panther God Nekara, Guardian of the Green. The great black beast seemed to stare down at her, almost watching in judgement as Selia bent low, groping for the blade that would call forth his power and set her free. Selia tried to smile as her fingers wrapped about the hilt of the blade. Pain racked her body as she tried to rise, one hand still braced on the statue for support.

Her head swam with the effort and she gasped.

Doubled over in agony she called on Nekara to guide her, for the Earth Mother to give her strength. Every pain, everything she did was for the Green. It was only right that the gods aid her now after all that she had done. As she had struggled so hard. For them!

It was all for them.

Gloria Swann felt the final knot loosen and fall away as she finally pulled on the rope with all her strength. The cords slipped free, her fingers guiding the rope in and out and around and soon she was pulling her bruised and bleeding wrists from the loose coils. Moaning into her gag, Gloria forced her aching arms forward and pushed herself up. Her legs were still bound, she knew, but the Queen of the Amazons was right in front of her, the knife in her hands once again. The warrior woman was obviously in agony though, struggling to rise as she clawed her way up the side of the massive statue.

Gloria knew she had little time before the Amazon would be after her again. Gloria spun about on her butt, putting her legs in front of her to attack the ropes that held her ankles together. She watched the woman before her and actually jumped, startled when the queen cried out. Gloria's eyes went wide with horror as she stared at the other woman's face. The last of the skin on the queen's face had melted away, and a grinning, leering skull stared back at her framed by wispy strands of black, grizzled hair. The eyes rattled in the deep, dark sockets. Her tongue flailed about in jaws barely held in place by thin strips of muscle. Her long, thick hair fell away as whatever was eating at her flesh dissolved her skin more with every second, rolling down her throat. Gloria screamed in stark terror, pushing back and away as the woman lurched forward. In desperation, Gloria kicked out, just wanting the grisly creature to stay away.

Angela Morgan looked up as Gloria's terror stricken scream filled the cavern, her concentration broken. She had given up on trying to pull the chains loose from their moorings atop the totem pole. As old and rusted as they were, they were still too strong to break or pull free. All that she had managed to do was make her wrists slick with sweat and blood. She had thought that that might help, as the manacles had been made for a person bigger than she was, but she could only force her hands through the metal cuffs to her knuckles and no further.

Angela had watched as the Amazon had shambled across the cavern seemingly more dead than alive. She was making her way for the knife, obviously, and Angela began struggling, straining her arms and legs to kick at the blade, which was just tantalizingly out of her reach. Her feet scraped against the ground kicking uselessly at rocks and gravel. Then, miraculously she spied something thin and sparkling in the firelight. It was golden, a needle of some sort. A stick pin she thought, used to adorn a cloak or robe in ancient times.

Angela's mind had raced as she glanced at Gloria still struggling with her own bonds. The aging star had loosened the ropes about her wrists but had yet to free herself, and the Amazon was almost within reach of the knife. Angela knew what she had to do. It would hurt, but she had little choice.

She placed her foot over the ornament and carefully dragged it closer through the dirt. It slipped free twice, but finally she had it within easy reach of both of her feet, turning it about in a position that she thought best. She looked up as the queen slumped against the huge statue of the man-cat, then bit down on the gag against the pain to come. She stepped down on the head of the pin, forcing the sharp tip up, then rammed her already sore foot onto the jewelry, hoping that the point would not find her flesh.

Angela moaned as the tip drove into the soft arch of her foot. She tried to ignore the pain however, immediately forcing her leg up, her fingers groping for the pin as tears welled in her eyes and ran down her cheeks. It took several tries, kicking higher each time, as she did not have the strength to hold up her leg for any length of time. Finally though she managed to grab her heel and hold her leg straining upright in place then grasped the pin between her slick fingers with enough pressure to get a grip. She gasped as it slid from her foot and boot, and she almost blacked out. It was too much. She held on though, with her life as well as Gloria's at stake; watching as the Amazon woman bent down finally to retrieve the lost blade. Angela rammed the pin into the key hole on the left manacle and frantically started digging into the locking mechanism.

It had been months since she had practiced escaping from hand cuffs and picking locks, but the skill came back to her in a rush. She felt the archaic tumblers push aside at her efforts and she smiled around her gag, almost whimpering in ecstasy. The manacles were not built to hold anyone for long, apparently, rather just for a time, before the captive was sacrificed to the statue. They were simple, old and rusty but simple, and Angela felt a snap as the first unlocked and fell away. Angela had let out a deep breath that she had not even realized she had been holding, then transferred the pin to her free hand to set to work on the other manacle, ignoring the raw and bloody scars about her wrists. It was then that she had heard Gloria's scream and looked up.

The Amazon's face had all but dissolved completely away, exposing most of her skull. Angela gasped, wondering how the woman was still alive as she clutched the blade in her shaking hand. The Amazon struggled though, trying to find the strength to plunge the knife into Gloria. The movie star was scrambling back, inching away as Angela reached out, trying to grab the queen from behind. The Amazon lurched forward then, and whether by panic or instinct Gloria kicked out with her bound legs trying to save herself.

Gloria Swann's kick connected with the Amazon Queen's hand, driving the knife back and away. Angela heard a ghastly shriek as the blade was driven into the woman's chest. Her face snapped up, the tongue lolling, wagging in the force of the queen's death gasp. Dead eyes stared, rolling in the hollow sockets as blood spewed forth, erupting unimpeded from the depths of the warrior's throat. Angela felt the sizzling blood as it spattered her own face as the woman staggered and spun away. She heard Gloria whine as it hit her as well, but she ignored the star's protests, more intent on the dying woman.

The queen staggered back, clutching at the hilt of the blade protruding from her chest. She fell against the statue, her fingers clawing desperately at the slick black stone. Angela stared, entranced as the woman slid down the monument, her jaws wagging as though she were trying to speak. The black stone glistened, streaked with blood as the woman fell in a heap at its base. The queen convulsed, twice, then collapsed to the dirt and lay still.

Gloria Swann stared, mesmerized as the Amazon Queen crumpled to the ground, dead, and all at once she collapsed herself. Exhaustion hit her like an anvil and she fell back gasping for breath. She could hear Angela, screaming through her gag, probably still terrified, but Gloria ignored the girl's cries. They were safe, and free, if not in body then in spirit. The Queen of the Amazons was dead, and Gloria Swann had saved the day.

Gloria sighed, content. It would be a simple matter to undo the bonds about her ankles now. She reached up lazily and pulled the gag down about her neck, then plucked the filthy wadded up cloth from her mouth. She did not even bother to untie the rag, more intent on working her jaw loose again. It felt wonderful.

"Gloria!"

Gloria Swann opened her eyes, irritated that the Morgan girl would not leave her be. Couldn't she just relax for a few minutes and let her regain her strength? They were both tired and hurt, but a few more minutes in chains would not hurt the little bit...

Gloria gasped and rolled to the side as the Amazon warrior drove the spear into the ground where she had just been laying. Gloria had totally forgotten the other, and now that woman was intent on killing her, completing the evil that her queen had started, or just for vengeance maybe. Gloria rolled back as the woman pulled the spear free, leaping over the movie star's feeble attempt to trip her up.

The Amazon warrior slammed her foot down into Gloria's stomach and Gloria felt her breath rush from her lungs. Her head swirled, her vision graying at the edges as she struggled for breath. She felt the woman's foot holding her down, and try as she might, Gloria could not gather the strength to fight back. She heard the Amazon's cry of rage. She saw the woman raise the spear high, the sharpened head glittering in the torchlight. Gloria screamed!

Angela Morgan screamed as she watched the Amazon warrior rushing across the cavern. She cried out for Gloria to move as the woman snatched up a spear from the floor and drew closer, anger creasing her beautiful face. Finally Angela had wit enough to pull her gag loose, but it was too late. Still, she screamed Gloria's name hoping for the best.

She watched as Gloria suddenly rolled to one side, avoiding the Amazon's thrust. The spear chucked into the dirt, and Gloria rolled back trying to trip the warrior, but the Amazon was too nimble and quick. She easily leaped over Gloria's attack and pulled her weapon free. She then pinned the star to the ground, planting a foot on Gloria's stomach and forcing the breath out of her.

Frantically Angela worked the stick pin into the lock of the other manacle still secured about her wrist. She was panicked though, her concentration spent as she watched the warrior raise her spear, prepared to strike. She felt the tumblers shift back into place and fall away as the thick cuff defied her. She glanced up, her attention divided between the manacle and Gloria. Was she going to be too late?

Something shifted in the shadows. Angela glanced up hearing the rough sound of stone grating against stone. Her brow wrinkled in confusion, her mind not believing what her eyes were seeing. She heard a slow, guttural growl, saw the long dark limbs of the statue start to shift and move.

Her eyes widened in horror as all at once the massive arm of the cat-man statue shot forward. Its sharp ivory claws glittered in the flickering torchlight as they raked up and across the back of the Amazon warrior. Angela saw the woman's eyes grow wide with surprise as she was lifted from her feet. The spear clattered to the floor as the force of the swift blow ripped the woman's back open and sent her sprawling far across the cavern. The huge cat-man howled, screaming in rage as it slowly, almost casually stepped down from its base, a massive tongue licking at its stone muzzle, stone grinding on stone.

Angela screamed, terror pouring from her throat. The cat-man statue was alive, somehow, some way. Its body rippled, but she did not know if it was muscles beneath the rocky skin or a trick of the light shining on the glossy stone. Its head shifted, moving back and forth as it scanned the cavern searching for prey. Its huge emerald eyes glistened in the torchlight, suddenly alight with intelligence. It was massive, imposing, like some dark god come down from the heavens. Some dark god of vengeance!

Angela saw the cat-man rear back, its gaze fixing on the woman at its feet. She saw the ivory claws slide free, extending from the black rock of its skin as the creature snarled, preparing to strike. To kill!

She heard someone scream, but she was not sure if the voice was Gloria's, or her own.

❋ ❋ ❋

EPISODE TEN:
LONG LIVE THE QUEEN!

Jennifer Higgins limped along, hurrying as best as she was able, trying to keep the fleeting form of Karl Braun in sight. Her ankle was killing her, sending a jolt of pain up her leg with every other ginger step that she took. She was hot and sweating, despite the relative coolness in the dank caves they were hurrying through. The humidity of the storm raging outside was oppressive however, making every breath, every step a new lesson in agony.

They had both survived the short fall down into the cavern hidden beneath the jungle floor. When the ground had given away, Karl had grabbed hold and twisted her about so that he would absorb most of the force of the impact, putting his own body under hers. They had not fallen too far, but far enough, and both were stunned when they had hit the dirty rock floor of the cavern that had been beneath them. They had lain there stunned, gasping for breath in the darkness as mud and debris had rained down about them. Jennifer did not know how long it had taken them to move, but it was Karl that had finally gotten her to her feet.

They had rested for a bit, just long enough to get their bearings and regain their lagging strength. They had fallen into a cavern she saw, a big cave that stretched far away into the darkness in all directions. Jennifer could hear running water, a river echoing somewhere in the distance, and the squeals of bats somewhere in the dark. She had shivered. Jennifer hated bats.

Before long, Karl had urged them on. The hole they had fallen through was far too high to reach again and climb out of, but he had surveyed the cavern while she had rested and found two slim tunnels leading, hopefully, out. Jennifer agreed that they had to get moving, to find some way out of the caves, so she leaned on Karl as he led the way, confident that he knew what he was doing.

Jennifer did not know how long they had been walking before they heard the first of the screams. It had seemed hours, and she was totally lost by then, turned all around in the confusing maze of dark, dank tunnels. More, she was aching and tired, and wanted nothing more than to collapse to the floor and curl up and sleep. Karl had kept her moving though. He seemed almost driven.

When the first scream had cut through the silence he had cursed, calling Angela's name automatically. Jennifer had tried to hang on as he hurried ahead, but he was determined and too fast, suddenly full of unbridled energy. He pulled free of Jennifer's grip, swiftly leaving her behind as she struggled to keep up. She could hear the clack of his heels echoing down the tunnel as he faded in and out of sight, rounding corners far ahead in the darkness. She called out for him to slow down, and soon started crying when she realized that he was not going to. He probably could not even hear her anymore.

Jennifer Higgins fell to the ground, stumbling and tripping in the dirty passage. She felt her knees scrape in the gravel again, ripping open old wounds from just hours before. She lay there in the darkness, sobbing, tired and sore as Karl Braun's footsteps faded away in the distance. She was alone.

She did not know just how long she lay there before she heard the screams again. It was women, she was sure, and they were terrified beyond belief from the sound of it. Jennifer snuffed back her tears, trying to sit up as she wondered what could scare someone so, suddenly worried that whatever it was might come for her as well.

She sat there in the darkness, cross-legged in the dirt, rubbing her injured ankle as she waited, hoping Karl would return. The screaming went on and on and at times she thought that she heard the sounds of a fight as well, the clank of metal. Terrified to be alone, it finally became too much and Jennifer cried out as well, clamping her hands over her ears, trying to silence the noise.

"Stop it!" she screamed, and again, "Stop it!"

After some time she lowered her hands again, and was miraculously greeted by silence. Somehow though, that seemed worse than the screams there in the lonely darkness. She waited, listening, wishing that Karl would come back for her.

Something clattered across the floor, bouncing off of the rocky walls, like stone striking stone. She glanced up, listening intently, but despite the time she had spent in the dark tunnels she still could barely see a few feet ahead of her. She heard what sounded like footsteps shuffling closer. She sighed, smiling weakly. It was Karl. It had to be.

"Karl?" she called out, then suddenly wished that she had not. The foot falls stopped. Jennifer listened, swallowing a lump in her throat, wondering suddenly why she had not heard the distinctive clack of Karl Braun's cowboy boots on the dusty stone floor of the cave.

Jennifer cursed, trying to rise without making too much noise. She winced as pain shot through her ankle, biting her tongue to keep from crying out. She staggered against the wall, trying to flatten against it. She suppressed a giggle thinking of the profile she was striking, trying to hide against the wall with her breasts sticking out and heaving with fear. It was absurd.

Something slammed into her, pushing her back against the wall. She felt her head loll back striking the rocky wall with enough force that she saw stars. She felt the breath rush out of her lungs with a 'huff'. She almost passed out, but hung on, clinging to consciousness, knowing that if she went out, she might never wake up again.

Dazed and confused, Jennifer felt a warm, sweaty body press up against her own, holding her in place against the wall. She wanted to scream as something cold and sharp was pressed into her throat, but she could barely draw a breath. She smelled foul breath as someone leaned in close, a shadow passing in front of her.

"Where is the man?" a voice hissed in her ear. Jennifer heard the harsh accent, like Spanish, but not quite, struggling with the English. Jennifer tried to answer, but her voice choked and broke, and all she emitted was a startled squeak. She felt the sharpness at her throat dig deeper. Something wet and warm trickled down her throat.

"Where, girl? Tell me!"

"I...I..." Jennifer tried to speak, but she was too afraid to gather her wits or her breath. She could just barely make out a female face before her own. It was little more than a pale patch in the darkness, but she could make out the dark eyes locked on her own, the cruel curl of lips just showing a hint of teeth. It was not Gloria, or the woman she had thought to be Gloria Swann before. That woman that had killed Alice Simmons and had tried to kill her as well. Would have killed her if not for Karl Braun. Now, however, Karl was no where about. Jennifer was alone with a madwoman that apparently wanted Karl, and probably her dead. Jennifer wanted to run. She wanted to scream or hide, but all she could do was stare wide-eyed into the darkness and babble.

Another scream echoed through the tunnels. Jennifer felt the woman's grip on her relax, felt the pressure of whatever sharp thing she held to her throat ease off if only slightly. Jennifer realized that this was probably the only best chance that she was going to get. The woman's attention was distracted, focusing on the fading scream. Jennifer drew her knee up with all of her might.

It was not as effective as it might have been against a man. Still, Jennifer knew that the area between a woman's legs was almost as tender, if only a little better protected. Her knee slammed up with enough force that she heard her attacker yelp in surprise and pain. Jennifer had actually lifted the woman up onto her toes with the force of the blow. She felt a knife tumble from the woman's hands as she came down and stumbled back, releasing her grip on Jennifer.

Jennifer knew that she had to press her advantage, so she screamed as loudly as she could and lunged forward. The bit actress, an Amazon extra in the latest Gloria Swann vehicle, thrust her arms out before her and charged. Her palms slapped against the fleshy mounds of her assailant, but Jennifer paid the strange sensation no heed. She pushed, feeling the woman stagger backward under the force of her shoving. Jennifer hoped to slam her attacker back against the far wall with enough force to knock her senseless. With a final, mighty thrust Jennifer heaved and promptly tripped over a jutting stone unseen in the dirt.

Jennifer Higgins fell to her knees again, sprawling onto the ground. She heard another shriek suddenly, a terrified yell that slowly faded away into nothing. Jennifer felt a chill wash over her as she suddenly realized that her outstretched arms were hanging over the edge of a cliff.

Jennifer eased herself forward, pulling her body up to the lip of the precipice. Slowly, cautiously she peered over the edge, surprised that she could even see. There was a faint glow far below illuminating a vast gorge. Jennifer could see the sparkling reflections of the river that she had heard before, rushing through the darkness. It seemed a raging torrent, even from her vantage, and was a deafening roar as she hung her head over to look. There was another cliff, and another trail on the far side of the gorge. If there was ever a way across, it must have long since crumbled away because Jennifer could not see it.

Jennifer backed away from the edge of the cliff, the realization of what she had just done slowly dawning on her. When she felt her foot touch the wall behind her, she curled up onto her knees and wrapped her arms tightly about herself. Tears filled her eyes and her throat started to close as she choked on her sobs. She had just killed a woman. She had just killed another human being. She had not meant to of course, but that did not matter. She had killed the woman, pushed her to her death.

Jennifer clamped her hands over her mouth, trying to hold back the screams of horror over what she had done. Her eyes grew wide, hearing the sound of the woman's own fading scream over and over in her mind. She had not seen the cliff in the darkness. Neither of them had. Jennifer gasped, a racking sob.

"Karl…" she choked.

What if Karl had not seen the cliff either?

Jennifer Higgins started to scream, then slumped back against the cool rocky wall and promptly fainted dead away.

Angela Morgan cursed as she jammed the golden stickpin she had found into the locking mechanism of the heavy manacle still firmly attached to her wrist. She was sweating bullets in the humid confines of the cavern, and panic rapidly rose and fell within her in rhythm to her fluttering heartbeat. Her eyes were wide as she bit into her lower lip, trying to concentrate. It was hard, what with Gloria Swann's constant, endless screeching.

"With a...mighty thrust, Jennifer heaved..."

She chanced a glance up again, cursing as she felt the pin slip off of the tumblers one more time. She sighed, breathing deeply, trying to calm down as she stared at the nightmare come to life, rampaging just a few feet away. It was still hard to believe. Angela believed in magic, but the more simple prestidigitations of the likes of Mandrake, and the escapology of Houdini. Giant statues that came to life were far beyond her humble imaginings and quite frankly horrifying.

Angela stared at the hulking creature, the massive obsidian statue of the cat-man come to life. It had been the last desperate ploy of the now dead Queen of the Amazons, a final spell that with her blood had caused the idol to stir and move. Angela did not know why the Amazon queen would go to such lengths, or why she hated them so. Perhaps she hated any that came to her land. Maybe she was just afraid and wanting her people to live in peace in the jungle, untouched by the outside world. Maybe that was how she maintained her rule; through fear. Whatever, the secret would never be revealed. The Queen of the Amazons had died bringing her beast to life, and it was now intent on fulfilling her final wish; killing them all!

Angela jammed the pin into the lock again, twisting until she felt the tumblers once more. She concentrated on the manacle, maneuvering the pin about inside the lock, but watching from the corner of her eye as the great beast stalked Gloria Swann across the vast dark chamber. Gloria was screaming to high heaven, scrambling through the dirt like a crippled mouse before a gigantic cat. Her ankles were still bound as the Amazons had tied her. She had not had the opportunity to catch a breath let alone free her legs. The giant cat-man seemed to know this and stalked Gloria, playing with her as any normal cat would its prey. Every time it seemed that Gloria might crawl beyond its clutches and escape, the creature would spring through the air, landing with a graceful thud blocking her path. Or it might simply snake its tail out to wrap about Gloria's legs, dragging her back within easy reach. Sometimes it simply batted her down, then waited for her to try and crawl away again. It was a sick little game, but the cat-man seemed to be enjoying it.

Angela had no doubts that the beast was watching her as well. Its eyes were emerald jewels, faceted like a fly's, and Angela was certain that it was not missing a trick. Which was why she did not try to hide what she was doing. She noted that the creature was always within a quick stride or two of her. She was sure that it was confident that she would not escape, even if she threw her leash, the confining manacle about her bloody, raw wrist.

Angela heard a click and felt the manacle finally loosen about her wrist.

She was careful not to show any elation. She showed no response in the fact that she was suddenly free, for in truth she was not. If she moved away from the totem, she was sure that the statue come to life would swat her down as it did Gloria over and over. It might tire of the game then, and kill them both on the spot. Still, she had to do something. Gloria was battered and bruised, and slowing down. And Angela saw that the star's eyes were wild and staring, her mind unable to come to grips with what was happening. Angela thought that her heroine might be going stark raving mad.

She watched as Gloria Swann scrambled through the dirt, trying in vain once again to crawl away from the stone beast. The creature watched as it had before, waiting, and at the last possible instant its tail snaked out from between its legs and wrapped about Gloria's bound ankles, dragging her back to it. It flung her back to the ground at its feet, cackling some cat laugh as it flicked a finger at her, making her squirm and squeal. Angela had to do something.

Screwing up her courage Angela charged forward, immediately wishing that she had not. She winced in pain as she stepped too hard on her twisted ankle, then gasped as she staggered forward, bending low to pick up the spear of the fallen Amazon; the first victim of the cat statue. Angela glanced across the chamber, spying the crumpled body of the Amazon warrior lying dead against the far wall that the creature had flung her into. She felt no pity, really, as the woman had been intent on killing she and Gloria, but still…

Angela ran forward, holding the spear high and trying to ignore the pain. Her ankle was throbbing. Her shoulder was bloody and raw from where the Amazon had shot an arrow just hours before. Her wrists were chafed and bleeding from her struggles against the rusting manacles. She was hot and exhausted and just wanted it all to be over. But she had to help Gloria.

The creature snarled, watching as she ran towards it. It still held Gloria to the ground, crouching as though about to attack, but its emerald eyes were focused on Angela limping across the cavern carrying a spear. Gloria kept screaming and squirming in terror, though not really trying to get away. The movie star feebly beat her fists on the creature's arms, but it ignored her best efforts. It seemed to eye Angela with amusement.

Faster than she could follow the cat thing swatted her aside. It was like being hit by a sledgehammer she imagined as she was suddenly flying across the cave. Her arm went numb from the blow, but she somehow managed to hold onto the spear with her other hand. This gave her some comfort and satisfaction as she slammed against the wall. She saw stars, stars that slowly faded to splotches of gray as she bounced off of the wall and on top of the body of the broken Amazon. That final fright was the only reason she did not immediately fade away into unconsciousness.

Gloria Swann shrieked as panic welled up within her once again. Through a haze of madness she saw the Morgan girl go flying across the cave and smash against the wall like a bird hurtling into a window. The creature had simply swatted her aside, then snarled its delight before turning its burning gaze back on Gloria. It was horrible. Horrible!

Gloria screamed again and the cat thing leaned in close, growling in her face, showing her a mouthful of jagged teeth. She did not feel its breath, though she thought she should have. It was unbelievable, and she could not begin to comprehend how such a thing could be. Gloria's mind drifted back as she considered the cat creature considering her. She had done a film once; Attack of the Zombies or some such drivel. In it however there had been something called a Golem in the script; a statue given life. Real life it seemed was imitating art.

Then suddenly it was clear. As clear as crystal, or emeralds at least. Gloria giggled with the sudden simplicity, remembering that two-bit movie some twenty years before. The Golem in the film had had a weakness; a jewel that was imbedded in its forehead. The cat creature had two similar jewels, emeralds for eyes.

Gloria squirmed, beating on the monster's arm as it leaned in close once more bearing ivory fangs in a fearsome snarl. Gloria's eyes went wide, thinking maybe that she had pushed the beast too far that time, but it just hunkered close, toying with her, scaring her. Gloria swallowed, and in a flash of utter foolishness she reached up, snatching one of the emeralds from its housing.

Angela snapped out of her daze hearing the creature's agonized howl. She stared wide-eyed, watching as the beast reared back, clutching at its eye and staggering to the side. It smashed up against the totem that she had been chained to not so long before, lashing out blindly and shattering the old, solid wood with a forceful blow. Angela watched as it howled again, then lowered its paw. It was trying to focus, but Angela saw that it was having a hard time, and with good reason. One of its emerald eyes was missing.

Angela sat up, her head reeling with pain as she looked about, trying to figure out what had happened. The creature was staggering, howling and lashing out at empty air. She saw Gloria crawling away as quickly as her arms would drag her. The monster seemed to ignore her at last, too intent on its own pain. Angela saw something in Gloria's hand as well, something green that sparkled in the torchlight, but for just a moment it did not connect. Gloria entered the circle of rain then, pouring down through the opening high above in the center of the cavern's dome-like roof. Outside lightning flared and the green in her hand caught the light, suddenly exploding in a dazzling brilliance. It was the emerald, Angela realized. The cat's eye!

The creature shrieked and shambled forward, straight for the sudden light, and Gloria! Angela struggled to her feet, her every movement agony. She braced against the slick rock wall, using the spear as a crutch, trying to stand. She heard the cat thing's anger, felt the ground tremble with every step it took.

"Gloria!" she shouted, staggering forward, knowing that she would never reach the star in time. "Throw away the jewel, Gloria! The emerald!"

The creature reared back, claws extended, ready to strike!

Angela screamed! Gloria screamed! The creature screamed…

There was a flurry of motion and suddenly Angela saw that someone had run forward out of the shadows and leaped onto the creature's back. The cat-thing snarled, reaching back to claw at the new attacker. It staggered into the fading circle of light, and only by blind luck managed to avoid crushing Gloria as she stared up in horror, too stricken to move.

Angela Morgan ran forward as fast as she could, ignoring the pain that shot through her leg with every step. Her shoulder pulsed as she hefted the spear, though what use it might be against the thing she had no idea. The monster flailed about, groping for the person on its back; the man clinging with his arms wrapped about the creature's throat. Angela gasped, feeling her heart rise into her throat.

"Karl…" she whispered, running forward all the faster.

It was Karl Braun, clutching to the creature's back like a maniac, hanging on for dear life. Karl Braun, Angela's mentor; the man that had taught her most of what she knew in the trade; stunts, acting, escapology. He had been like a father to her for more years than she cared to count. More of a father than her own had been able to be. Angela shrieked.

"Karl!"

She saw Karl Braun's gaze turn her direction, and just for a moment their eyes locked. She saw the love, the delight in the knowledge that she was still alive. He must have thought she had died in her fall from the biplane, the stunt that had been sabotaged by the Amazons. They all thought that she was dead. That was why no one had found her, or even come looking for her. No one but Karl.

Angela screamed and fell to her knees as she saw the creature reach back and rake its claws across the width of Karl's back. Karl cried out in agony as his eyes rolled up into his head. Angela saw his grip about the monster's neck falter, but with his last ounce of strength he managed to barely hold on. At least until the cat-thing reached back again.

The beast yelled its rage. Angela heard it but tried not to look, too afraid of what she might see. She forced her legs to start moving again, planting the butt of the spear into the dirt to lever herself up. She started running, faster and faster, ignoring again the pain in her ankle, the pains shooting all through her body. She could hear the cat-man raging. She could hear Karl's moans as he struggled to hold onto the beast, and Gloria's cries as she tried to get away. Angela hefted the spear in her hands and looked up, wishing she had not.

Gloria Swann had managed to scurry away and was finally unloosing the ropes coiled about her ankles. As soon as she was free, Angela knew that she would be up and running, and out of the way. Karl still clutched at the statue's neck and shoulders, but only just. Angela could see his strength fading, his face growing paler with the monster's thrashing about. The back of his shirt was soaked with blood, and Angela knew that he would not be able to hang on much longer. It was up to her then, and she had to hurry.

"Karl!" she shouted, charging right in front of the creature and brandishing the spear. "Let go, Karl! Jump off!" Angela jabbed up with the spear, wincing as the polished flint tip scraped across the slick black stone that was the beast's skin creating a shower of sparks. The monster turned its one-eyed gaze on her, snarling its annoyance, but otherwise unaffected. It swatted a massive paw at her, but she ducked, trying to deflect the blow with the spear over her head. The force of the swing almost tore the staff from her grip, and she felt the wood crack with the glancing blow.

"Engel," Karl cried out, his voice weak and cracking. Angela felt her heart skip a beat as she looked up, seeing the anguish on her old friend's face. "Run, Engel! Run!"

Angela watched on in horror as the beast snatched Karl Braun's limp form from its back. The stunt master's grip slipped free easily at the creature's tug, and all at once Karl was dangling in the grip of the beast trapped between its claws. She cried out, reaching for him, but the cat-thing ignored her pleas, throwing her mentor to the ground between them, like a rag-doll. Angela saw his body bounce, heard his bones shatter. Then in a flash, the creature smashed its paw down, driving its sharp claws through Karl Braun's chest, pinning him to the floor like a butterfly to a board. Angela heard Gloria's new fit of screams as she watched Karl's body convulse from the pain and shock. He coughed; spitting blood as the panther statue slipped its claws back out, ripping Karl's chest even more. Karl Braun coughed once again, then lay still.

Angela screamed her pain and loss, her anger spewing forth as she rammed the spear forward. She jabbed the spear up into the panther's face, trying to drive it back as she stepped across Karl's body trying to protect it. The creature roared, batting at the stick as it flailed about its face. Angela saw the monster's ears lay back, its muzzle wrinkling as it bared its fangs. It was done toying with them, she thought.

The monster lurched forward; dropping to all fours then sweeping at Angela, claws splayed. Angela blocked the panther's attack with the shaft of the spear, but the force of the blow splintered it in two and sent her flying back. She landed hard on her buttocks in the dirt, unseen bells ringing in her ears. The cat-thing reared above her, jaws wide, ready to strike.

Something snapped against the creature's stone skin, shattering on impact with enough force to give the beast pause. It looked up and about as another arrow bounced off of its rock-hard neck. Still, the cat-thing yowled, more annoyed than anything. Angela scrambled back; crab walking away as the panther sniffed the air, trying to find the new attacker. Angela craned her neck as another arrow bounced off the creature's hide, and finally saw Gloria Swann.

The movie star was across the temple chamber, standing where the Amazons had set up their makeshift camp. She looked an awesome, awful sight standing in her brassiere and silk slip, her hair a tangled matted mess, drawing back a long arrow on a short wooden bow. It was the very bow that the Amazon had used against Angela she guessed, the Amazon now dead against the wall of the cavern. Angela could see Gloria trembling as she let fly another shaft, and was surprised to see it strike its target. She had not missed yet, but unfortunately the arrows did little damage and only angered the beast. Still, any help was better than none.

Angela Morgan scrambled to her feet once again. She still had the two halves of the spear in her hands, but figured them to be useless. The cavern was littered with archaic weapons, however. It was simply a matter of finding one that she could lift and use. She cast a quick worried glance at the creature, crouching and batting at Gloria's arrows in annoyance. It eyed her, but was distracted as Angela cast her gaze about for a new weapon- another spear, or a sword.

"Angela!"

Angela looked up at Gloria's warning, just in time to see the cat-man pounce. It was in mid-air, almost upon her, its arms spread wide like one of the great jungle cats it emulated. Its ivory claws and fangs were truly dazzling in the torchlight, its one emerald eye crackling like fire. Angela cried out in a sudden panic and fell back. With pure survival instinct, she brought her hands up to shield her face as the creature dropped upon her. The claws slashed at her sides, her legs. She felt the creature's teeth as they grazed past her ear, snagging in her hair. Its growl deafened her, its hulking stone mass covering her like a blanket, wrapping her in darkness.

"Angela..."

Angela Morgan gingerly opened her eyes. The light was dim, the air still thick with the smells of smoke and incense, so she suspected that she was still in the cavern; the Amazon temple. But she was still alive, and of that she was surprised. She craned her neck, trying to focus on the soft sounds of the voice she heard and promptly moaned as her muscles protested the sudden movement.

"Oh, Angela. Thank god!"

Angela looked up and saw the laughing, tear-streaked face of Jennifer Higgins smiling down on her. She was crying, but happy tears of joy streaking the dirt that was dried and caked on her face. She looked a right mess.

"Lord, Jennifer," Angela croaked, coughing. "What happened to you?"

Jennifer grinned and leaned over her friend, giving her a tight squeeze that made Angela moan all the more. Angela suddenly gasped however, and sat up, pushing her friend aside.

"The panther!" she cried out, trying to get to her feet. Her abused and aching ankle gave way though, and she was soon back on her butt. She felt Jennifer's hand on her shoulder.

"Easy! Easy, Angela, it's dead." Angela followed where Jennifer was pointing and saw the creature, or what was left of it. Gloria Swann was standing amidst the crumbled remains of the cat statue. In her hands she held one of the archaic weapons that had been littering the floor; a Spanish battle-axe, by the look of it. She was wielding it like a sledgehammer, striking the larger chunks of obsidian with all the force that she could muster, breaking up what was apparently left of the creature, turning it to gravel and dust. Angela was confused.

"What...what happened?" Angela looked at Jennifer, hoping for an answer, but her friend simply shrugged.

"I stumbled in here just at the last of all the action. That thing was attacking you. I thought it was gonna rip you to pieces. I started to run forward when I saw Gloria over there with a bow." Jennifer pointed. "She fired an arrow and it hit that thing right in the head. It screamed, and grabbed at its eye about the same time I saw you ram a stick at it. Then it just seemed to tremble and break apart. It collapsed right on top of you. Me and Gloria ran over to help, to dig you out, and we dragged you over here. Then Gloria picked up that axe and started bustin' the thing up into little pieces. I never heard nobody curse like that, lemme tell you."

Angela stared at the movie star for a moment. The woman had more gusto than she had given her credit. Gloria Swann looked a filthy mess, covered in dirt, dripping in sweat, but right then she looked awesome as well, and Angela remembered why the woman had been her heroine growing up.

"Karl..."

Jennifer shook her head with a frown. "He's dead, Angela. I'm sorry. Alice too. Karl and I found her, mauled to death. We thought that Gloria had done it. We saw her, but then Karl said that it wasn't her. I'm confused..."

"Me too, Jenn..." Angela said, leaning back and trying to rest, relax. "Me too."

It had taken the three women the better part of that night to walk back to the plateau and the film camp. They had tended their wounds and cleaned up as best they could in the water supply that the Amazon warriors had left behind. It had not taken long for them to find their way from the caverns with no one chasing them, and as it turned out, Jennifer had been only a few yards from an exit where she had fought and killed the final Amazon.

Jennifer had told her friends of her travails in the jungle as well as in the caves. How she had come upon the Amazon Queen, still disguised as Gloria, in the act of killing poor Alice Simmons. How Karl Braun had saved her, but then how they had both fallen into the caves. She told how Karl had run ahead upon hearing the screams of Angela and Gloria, and how she had then pushed the Amazon warrior over the cliff in the tunnels after a short but fierce struggle. Angela could tell that Jennifer was upset over that, and she and Gloria both tried to comfort her, and told her that it was not her fault. The Amazons had been trying to kill them in the end, and it was self-defense. That eased Jennifer's conscience a bit, but Angela knew that what Jennifer had done would haunt the girl till her dying day.

Angela and Gloria in turn told their tales on the long walk back to camp. Gloria, how she had been kidnapped, and how the Amazon Queen had then stolen her face to infiltrate the film company. Angela, and how she had survived the plunge from the biplane stunt only to become lost in the caverns. How the two women had met up, and their battles then with the Amazons and their disfigured queen, and finally the statue of the cat-man come to life. It sounded ridiculous as the three women swapped tales, like stories out of a dime novel or pulp magazine, but it passed the time. They mourned for Alice, and especially for Karl, and wished that they could have brought the bodies out of the jungle, but they were all just too tired and injured. They could barely carry themselves, and more often than not the three women were leaning on one another every step of the way.

It was dawn as the women trudged up the trail that ran up the side of the plateau. A bloated orange sun just topped the jungle canopy to the east, scarring the sky a bloody red. It would be storming again, probably that night, as it was the start of the rainy season in Brazil. The three women all hoped they would be away from the damned jungle soon.

The camp was just coming awake as they staggered within sight. Stagehands were up and about, stirring the dying fires and readying the morning meal. Angela saw Pitt fussing over his aeroplane far across the top of the plateau. They marched on, unobserved, and it was Jimmy Barton the camera operator, just coming out of the latrine, that finally spotted them.

"Holy cow!" he shouted, staring in disbelief as the three women trudged by him, ignoring his exclamations.

His shouts had stirred the camp however, and within moments the three women were surrounded by the cast and crew. They were battered with questions, probing hands trying to support them and help them on the final leg of their journey, the last few yards. They were all filthy and smelling, and tired beyond endurance. Jennifer wanted nothing more than to collapse onto her cot in her tent and sleep for a week.

It was Kathy Parker, the crew nurse that finally brought some order to the mob surrounding the women. She had made the trek up the mountain the day before after Harkins had sent the small group of hands and editors back to the main camp to tell everyone what had happened. Kathy had them taken to her tent, sending Jimmy off to rouse Jonathan. She dragged Martha and Carol into her tent as well then ordered everyone else out while they tended to the women and their injuries. It took some time, even with Kathy directing Martha and Carol, to clean the women up properly and bandage their wounds with clean cloth, wrapping strained limbs and stitching deep cuts and scrapes. It was some fifteen minutes later when Jonathan Harkins burst into the nurse's tent.

"My god!" he grumbled upon seeing the three women. Angela and Jennifer were lying on cots, their legs splinted and tightly wrapped. Angela had bandages wrapped about her ribs and wrists as well, and her shoulder was swathed in rags and gauze. Kathy Parker was hunched over Jennifer, plucking dirt and gravel from the scabs on her knees. Gloria Swann was half submerged in a canvas tub of steaming water, Carol knuckling her aching back while Martha dabbed at the woman's wrists with alcohol. The tent was filled with cigarette smoke.

"Where the devil have you three been?" Jonathan snapped, striding into the tent, ignoring Gloria's nakedness. "We've all been worried sick!"

"What?" Angela started to rise, but Kathy held her back.

"Jonathan.."

The director waved the nurse off, wanting her to be silent. He turned, leveling a finger at Gloria Swann. "You, Gloria! You should know better. Why you went charging off into the jungle when we had shots to complete, I'll never know. Now where's Braun, and the Simmons girl? I suppose we'll have to wait on their sweet return, eh?"

"Karl's dead, Jonathan. So's Alice." Gloria stared at the director coolly, taking a drag off of her cigarette before tossing it aside. She stood up in the old canvas wash tub, water dripping from her naked, bruised body and looked Harkins up and down with disgust. He seemed dumbfounded, thinking perhaps that he should have come into the tent with a bit more concern. Still...

"Well, I'm sorry for that, but we still have a film to finish, Gloria. Your film! You told me that no matter what we would finish this-"

"It is finished, Jonathan. It's over." Gloria Swann stepped shakily from the tub, accepting the towel that Martha handed her and quickly dried herself. "We'll take what we have and make do. Too many people have paid the price for my vanity. De Grassi, Alice, Karl... that's enough. More than it should have been."

"Gloria…" Harkins pleaded. "Don't be stupid. We can turn this all around. We can…"

"You're fired, Jonathan." Gloria Swann shrugged into a rain slicker offered by Martha as the other women in the tent stared on in open-mouthed disbelief. Angela had sensed that the movie star had changed since their shared adventure, but she had never expected this.

Harkins blinked. "You can't fire me!"

"I can, Jonathan. And I just did. Read your contract. I have final say on all matters. Everything! We are going to take what we have and get the hell out of this damned jungle. Swann Productions will put together what we have into something that will get us some money, but as far as filming, this movie is done." Gloria Swann lit another cigarette and took a long drag, staring all the while at Harkins.

Jonathan Harkins, one of Hollywood's most respected directors looked about the tent, meeting in turn the gaze of each of the six women gathered there and knew that he was totally alone. He sighed, not being a total fool, and turned to leave, but as he was about to duck under the tent flap he glanced back at the high and mighty Gloria Swann.

"You can't get away with this, Gloria. You'll hear from my lawyers!" And then he was gone.

The tent was silent for a long moment, none of the women quite sure what to say. It was Gloria, oddly, who finally broke the silence.

"Prick!" She smirked, then looked at the others.

"Ladies, I do need a drink…"

Mann's Chinese Theater
Hollywood, California
1936

It was one of the coldest nights on record, and the weathermen were actually considering snow in the forecast. A light rain was falling and a chill wind whistled through the streets whipping loose papers into the air and swirling coat tails and skirts alike. Still, the bitter weather did little to dampen the excitement of the crowd that had gathered outside of Mann's. They pushed forward against the velvet ropes lining the sidewalk, ignoring the angry shouts of the police that had been called in to hold them at bay. Each and every one was near frenzied, all hoping to catch a glimpse of one of Hollywood's greats.

There was a shout followed by a roar of cheers as the ushers stepped forward and wedged the gilded glass doors of the fanciful movie house open wide. The crowd surged again as the Press moved forward and sharply dressed movie attendants filed out to line the red carpet. And then, Gloria Swann, star of stage and screen, the Leading Lady of Tinsel Town adventure serials stepped out of the theater and turned her fur collar against the unseasonable chill.

The glare of flash bulbs exploded about her as she smiled, waiting for Adam Kaine to catch up with her. Off to one side she saw the newsreel cameras cranking and she waved happily, flashing her million-dollar smile. She was dressed to the nines; her long mink brushing along the red carpet they had laid for her premiere, her hair coifed just so, accentuated with the most stylish and fashionable cap. Her hands were sheathed in the finest black kid leather, and she waved, showing off the gloves for her fans, those few that lived to see her and what she wore. They cheered, of course, the velvet ropes and security barely holding back the hundreds that had turned out to see her latest, final epic.

The Queen of Escapes was a success. The crowds in the theater had cheered when they were supposed to, and laughed and cried. They had shown the entire serial in one setting, editing together the ten episodes back to back into one non-stop thrill ride that had lasted almost five hours. The fans had loved it. The critics had seemed pleased, jotting down notes in their little black books, and careful not to miss a moment of the action. There was applause when the final credits rolled, after she and Kaine had kissed, flying off into the setting sun. They had risen to their feet when they saw the final dedication to Alice Simmons, and Karl Braun, the greatest stunt master that had ever lived. Gloria smiled. It had been a nice touch, the right thing to do.

Adam Kaine finally came up beside her, waving to the crowd and smiling amidst another roar and explosion of flashing lights. Truly, he had had very little to do in the movie, just a cameo appearance really, but he had a name, and he drew in the young girls and boys. He had been needed, and he was paid well if only for his name. He would have another hit to add to his list when the serial was released nation wide for Thanksgiving. There would be no awards, of course, but he would get his money, and his fame. They all would, though it no longer really mattered. Gloria had what she wanted, all that she needed, for herself as well as the others.

Adam Kaine took her arm and Gloria allowed him to walk her down the carpet towards the awaiting limousines. It was tradition, the star and starlet arm in arm walking through the crowds after the premiere. They waved and smiled, waved and smiled, almost going blind in the explosion of flash bulbs. When they reached the end of the red carpet, Adam kissed her hand, as was expected, then waited to help her into her car.

Gloria turned as a cheer went up through the crowd again, suspecting somehow that it was not for her. Just coming out of the theater, at the lead of the lesser cast members she saw Angela. Angela Morgan looked beautiful, and Gloria sighed, seeing herself as she had been over a decade before. She was young, her hair styled fashionably, the white lock on her brow no longer hidden by a cheap theatrical rinse. She wore a gown that accentuated her bright green eyes, her own fur coat open to the cold night air. She had snagged Crabbe for her escort, as she was slated to be his leading lady in his next space adventure serial, 'Flash' something or other. Her first starring role. Gloria was pleased. She deserved it after all her hard work. After all that she had been through. Gloria waved to Angela, waved and smiled.

Angela saw and waved back, her own smile shining brightly. She had given Angela full credits in the film, the gentle nudge that the girl had needed to get her career going. The crowd had loved her, and cheered to see her name at the end of the movie. Gloria saw the starlet wink and finger a small pendant she had taken to wearing; a little chip of emerald set in gold. There were only two others like it in the world, cut from one of the two largest emeralds ever brought out of the South American jungles. Gloria had the second necklace, and the third belonged to a young woman named Higgins who had returned and retired to St. Louis with Gloria Swann's good graces.

Gloria Swann smiled knowingly, and with a final wave to her fans turned and slipped into the rear compartment of her limousine. Kaine started to climb in after her, but she waved him back, dismissing him. She did not need him anymore. He looked a little shocked, but knew better than to complain as he backed out of the car and shut the door. She was Gloria Swann, after all.

Gloria Swann, the Queen of Escapes!

—The End—

❀ ❀ ❀

Credits:

The Cast:

Gloria Swann.........................The Queen of Escapes
Adam Kaine...........................The Hero
Alice Simmons.......................First Amazon
Martha Johnson.....................Second Amazon
Jennifer Higgins.....................Third Amazon
Joyce Needler........................Fourth Amazon
Ginger Sachs.........................Fifth Amazon

The Villains:

Selia.....................................El Gato Negra, the Black Cat
Beran....................................Amazon Spear Carrier
Dyla.....................................Amazon Archer

The Crew:

Joseph Hunt..........................First Camera
Jimmy Barton........................Second Camera
Jackson Walters......................Editor
Phil Turner............................Inside Prop
Kathy Parker..........................Company Nurse
Carol Page.............................Make-up
Shirley Compton.....................Script
Bill De Grassi........................Stagehand/Prop Handler
Trent....................................Stagehand/Prop Handler
Karl Braun.............................Stunt Coordinator
Angela Morgan.......................Stunt Woman
Sebastian Pitt........................Stunt Pilot
John Thomas..........................Assistant Director

Directed by Jonathan Harkins
A Swann Staiputt Production

ABOUT OUR CREATORS

Author:

CURTIS FERNLUND – was born May 15th, 1962 in Medford, Oregon, which is about 45 miles north of the California border. He grew up there with my parents and sister, raised there and went to school, worked and played until 1984 when he loaded a U-Haul with most of his worldly belongings and drove cross country with three of his friends, eventually settling in Brooklyn, New York. A few years after he met his soul mate, Erica, and moved to Manhattan to live with her where they spent eighteen wonderful years together until her passing in 2006.

Moving to New York City, he was hoping to get a career in the comic book industry as an artist, but he reached a peak in his drawing skill and could not seem to improve enough to surpass it. He turned his focus to writing then as he had have always been a fan of the older Pulp genre and a role-play gamer. He has dozens but was only professionally published Airship 27 accepted his first short story, 'Kiri: Night of the Mist' published in Mystery Men (& Women) Volume III.

This is only his second published work and his first novel, again thanks to Airship 27, and a couple friends. One in particular not only inspired his passion for writing again, but helped him through the very dark times after his girlfriend's passing.

Interior Illustrator:

JAMES E. LYLE - is a native of western North Carolina, having been born in Asheville in 1963 and raised in the mountains near Waynesville. In the sixth grade he decided that being an artist was what mainly interested him. James has been a professional cartoonist and illustrator for the past thirty years, working primarily as a freelance but occasionally dabbling in full-time employment.

He has been published by such companies as Acclaim/Valiant Comics, Caliber Comics, Now Comics, and Zenescope Entertainment. He contributed a number of illustrations to the Weekly Reader line of magazines, he has created illustrations for Jones Soda Co., Ron Jon Surf Shop, J.C. Penny Apparel and other major companies. James has also designed CD art for recording artists like Todd Rundgren and Sloug Feg. He also finds time to give private art lessons, creates commissioned artwork, and also plays music with Gypsy Bandwagon.

In 2013 James was elected Chairman of the Southeast Chapter of the National Cartoonists Society after serving two terms as Vice-Chair to that group. James still lives near Waynesville with his wife, Karin.

Cover Painter:

ANDY FISH - Fish is a writer and artist of graphic novels and comic books. He has a lifelong passion for serials and pulp magazines which is why he is thrilled to be providing art and covers for Airship 27. His latest graphic novel, DRACULAS ARMY from McFarland Press is being released during the Halloween 2013 season. Andy is delighted to be working with the Airship 27 team. You can visit his website at - www.andytfish.com

Here be Ghosts

Situated in the rural back country of Edwardian England is an old, mysterious house whose unique owner earns his living as a Spirit-Breaker, a hunter of ghosts. A former military veteran, **Sgt. Roman Janus** has devoted his life to aid those haunted, both emotionally and physically by obsessive wraiths whose spirits are still anchored to our world.

Airship 27 Productions is thrilled to present *Sgt. Janus – Spirit Breaker* by Jim Beard. Part detective, part occultist, Janus is himself a man of mystery whose own past is shrouded and the motivations behind his calling kept hidden. Within this volume you will find eight tales as narrated by his clients, each with his or her own perspective on this uncanny hero and his amazing career. Filled with suspense, terror and agonizing pathos, each a solid mesmerizing journey into the unknown world beyond.

JIM ANTHONY
SUPER-DETECTIVE

He's half Comanche, half Irish and ALL AMERICAN!! Jim Anthony the Super Detective returns in his fourth volume of brand new adventures from Airship 27 Productions.

Traveling the globe, Anthony battles all manner of twisted villainy in four new tales and his challenges are herculean. Writers Erwin K. Roberts, Joel Jenkins, Frank Byrns and Mark Justice have whipped up a quartet of high adventure stories that are the hallmark of the Super Detective. From Mexico, where he encounters a Nazi spy ring to the streets of Manhattan where he hunts down a brutal serial killer, Jim Anthony proves once again why he is one of the most exciting and fun heroes ever created in the golden age of American pulps.

This volume, the fourth in an on-going series, features interior illustrations by Michael Neno and a dazzling cover by Eric Meador, with book designs by Rob Davis. Airship 27 Productions is thrilled to continue the exploits of the one and only, Jim Anthony – Super Detective.

PULP FICTION FOR A NEW GENERATION!

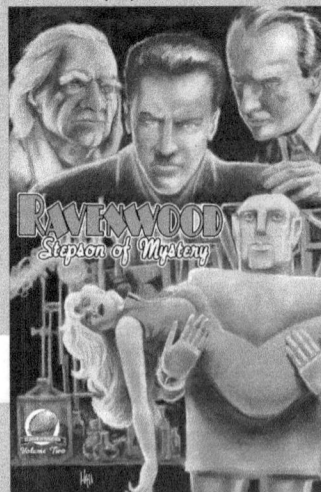